Ristéard's Unwilling Empress:
Lords of Kassis Book 4

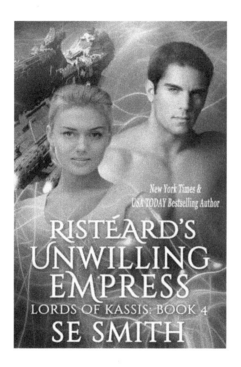

By S.E. Smith

Acknowledgments

I would like to thank my husband Steve for believing in me and being proud enough of me to give me the courage to follow my dream. I would also like to give a special thank you to my sister and best friend, Linda, who not only encouraged me to write, but who also read the manuscript. Also to my other friends who believe in me: Julie, Jackie, Lisa, Sally, Elizabeth (Beth) and Narelle. The girls that keep me going!

—S.E. Smith

Montana Publishing
Science Fiction Romance
Ristéard's Unwilling Empress: Lords of Kassis Book 4
Copyright © 2015 by S.E. Smith
First E-Book Published February 2015
Cover Design by Melody Simmons

ALL RIGHTS RESERVED: This literary work may not be reproduced or transmitted in any form or by any means, including electronic or photographic reproduction, in whole or in part, without express written permission from the author.

All characters, places, and events in this book are fictitious or have been used fictitiously, and are not to be construed as real. Any resemblance to actual persons living or dead, actual events, locales, or organizations are strictly coincidental.

Summary: Grand Ruler Ristéard needs Ricki, she is the Great Empress foretold as their world's savior, and he can't allow her to keep her distance for long.

ISBN: 978-1-942562-61-0 (paperback)
ISBN: 978-1-942562-24-5 (eBook)

Published in the United States by Montana Publishing.

{1. Science Fiction Romance – Fiction. 2. Science Fiction – Fiction. 3. Paranormal – Fiction. 4. Romance – Fiction.}

www.montanapublishinghouse.com

Synopsis

Ristéard Roald is the powerful and deadly ruler of Elpidios, a planet that is slowly dying without the Blood Stones needed to absorb the radiation gradually destroying its stratosphere. He has sworn to do whatever it takes to protect his world and his people, but time is running out.

Hope comes from an unexpected source, the Kassis. They have found a way to replicate the Blood Stones needed to save his world, but his first dealings with a traitorous Kassisan has left a deep distrust for the species.

Ricki Bailey is used to dealing with diplomats and handling complex situations. After all, as the daughter of the owners of Cirque de Magik, the most spectacular Circus to the Stars, she is used to organizing their trips to foreign countries. Her life changes when her mother and father decide to take the circus to the real stars... and to another star system!

If she thought learning new laws and customs was going to be a challenge, it was nothing to the sudden interest she was getting from a huge blue male known as the Grand Ruler! Ricki discovers words that she didn't even realize were in her vocabulary, most of them not in the least polite.

She decides the best way to deal with the arrogant male is to treat him like she did when encountering difficult Consuls during the circus' travels on Earth; stay cool, calm, and professional and only deal with the facts necessary to complete whatever business transaction was required.

Ristéard is stunned when a strange, alien female, foretold in the ancient tablets as being the great Empress who will save his world, appears. He is even more astonished when she refuses his attentions! With the life of his planet at stake, not to mention his own peace of mind and body, he will do whatever is necessary to ensure the female stays by his side.

Yet, there are forces working against him and Ricki, powerful forces that do not want him to be successful. Dangers and traitors among his own council threaten not only him, but her. It will take all of Ristéard's resources, and a few unexpected allies, to complete the dangerous journey ahead of them.

Can he keep his unwilling Empress safe from those that would destroy her? Better yet, can he save his world when there are those that would destroy it for the treasure of precious Blood Stones hidden somewhere beneath its surface?

Contents

Chapter 1
Earth: Twenty-four years before.

The figure dressed in black slipped around the darkened trailer that was attached to the large truck. He held the parcel tightly against his chest, as if afraid that it might disappear. He paused when he heard the sound of a cough coming from the large tent followed by several voices. The bundle in his arms moved slightly, jerking his attention back to his mission.

He didn't have much time. Stepping up to the trailer, he gently laid the tightly wrapped bundle on the step. For a brief moment, his hand hovered over the pale cheek. Sorrow and regret pulled at him, two foreign emotions that he had never felt before.

"Be safe, my daughter, I will come for you when you are older if I can," the soothing deep voice whispered in a strange dialect.

His vivid blue eyes darkened with sadness as he pulled an envelope from his shirt and tucked it in the blanket before straightening. He stepped back into the shadows of the trailer when the sound of the voices grew closer. It would be dawn soon and he needed to leave before it became light enough for him to be seen by the figures beginning to move around the clustered group of motorhomes.

He had just stepped behind the side of the trailer when he heard the door to it open. A slow, startled gasp followed by a hushed cry swept through the air. Leaning back, he waited to see if he had made the right decision.

"Walter!" The sound of a woman called out. "Walter, come here!"

"What is it, Nema?" The deep voice of the man called Walter asked.

In his mind, he could almost see what the woman had discovered. The same pale, delicate skin, the same vivid golden hair, and the promise of his own blue eyes, the only thing that his daughter had inherited from him that was obvious. Clenching his fists, he forced his body to remain still, silent, as he waited to see if they would accept the precious gift he had laid at their door.

"It's a baby," Nema whispered, her voice full of tears. "Isn't she beautiful, Walter?"

"Now, Nema," Walter started to say before his voice faded. "What's this?"

The faint beam of a light came on followed by the whisper of paper. For a moment, only the faint sounds of a dog barking in the distance and the low-pitch croaking of frogs from a nearby pond broke the silence.

"What does it say?" Nema quietly asked.

"Please keep our daughter safe," Walter murmured. "She needs a loving home where she can be accepted for who she is. Her name is Ricki. I give my heart to you to hold and protect… Please, care for her as if she was your own."

"Oh, Walter," Nema sniffed. "She's beautiful, we have a daughter, a beautiful daughter of our own."

"Nema...," Walter started to say before he stopped with a sigh. "She is beautiful, just like you. We're leaving in just a couple of hours."

"We aren't going to...," Nema whispered hesitantly as she gazed down at the sleeping infant in her arms.

"No, I know of an attorney who can take care of the paperwork," Walter replied in a gruff voice.

"Ricki," Nema said tenderly. "Ricki Rose Bailey."

"Nema," Walter said.

"Rose wouldn't mind," Nema replied. "She would have loved having a baby sister named after her. I know she is looking down on her now and smiling with pride."

"Ricki Rose is a beautiful name," Walter replied in a tight voice as he thought of the beautiful daughter that they had lost a year ago at birth. He had come close to losing Nema as well. She had to have emergency surgery to prevent her from bleeding to death. As a result, they would never have the child that they had dreamed of. His fingers trembled as he hesitantly reached out to touch the sleeping infant's cheek. When he looked up, he saw the hope, fear, and tears in his beloved wife's eyes. "Just as beautiful as you are, Nema. I love you."

Nema looked up and smiled. "I love you, too, Walter," she whispered before she tsked. "Can you see if Mary has any formula? I need to get the things we had for Rose out. Oh, Walter, we have a little girl!"

Walter gazed up at Nema's tiny figure. At barely over three and a half feet tall, she looked more than a child from the back. He appeared to tower over her at four feet one inch. A sigh escaped him as he thought of the two boxes hidden in the back of their bedroom closet. She had refused to let him give the baby gifts away, saying she wasn't ready to let go. He knew she hoped they would one day adopt a baby, but he had doubts that any judge would allow them to.

It wasn't because of the fact they were both dwarves, but because of their life style. As owners of the Cirque de Magik, a small, but unique circus filled with unique characters from around the world, they were constantly on the move. He had taken every bit of money he had inherited and earned during his own life as a member of the circus to buy this show from its previous owners in the hope of making it one of the best shows ever seen.

A slow smile lit his face when he heard Nema singing softly. "I'm a father," he chuckled. "We have a daughter."

* * *

The figure standing in the shadows moved silently away as the door closed. The tightness in his chest eased slightly as he strode away from the roadside show he had discovered earlier. He had spent most of the day listening and watching from a distance. Deep down, he knew that this was the most promising place for keeping his daughter safe from those that would kill her like they had her mother.

He paused for just a brief moment to look at the strange collection of tents, trailers, and carnival sideshow exhibits one last time before he turned.

Where he was going was no place for an infant. He did not see the two men studying him as he disappeared into the early morning mist.

Chapter 2

Ristèard touched the blood seeping from the cut along his cheek with the back of his left hand. His eyes narrowed on the two men and one woman that were circling him. Shifting the blade in his right hand, he pressed the button hidden in the handle.

His left hand dropped, catching the second blade as it separated from the first. Swirling around when the woman snarled at him and stepped forward, he sliced the blade in his left hand across her neck before continuing the circle to run the blade in his right hand across the upper thigh of one of the males.

Satisfaction coursed through him when the male dropped to the ground as he sliced through muscle, tendons, and veins. The male grabbed at his leg in a desperate bid to stem the blood pouring from the gaping wound. Ristèard knew the strike had cut through the femoral artery and the assassin would bleed to death in minutes without immediate medical attention.

"Who sent you?" Ristèard demanded as he circled the other assassin.

The male just shook his head and grinned, never taking his eyes off of him. He jerked back, blocking the blow when the man thrust his arm outward. A low curse escaped him when the blade of the sword suddenly extended and cut a long, shallow line along his neck.

Cold fury burned through his veins before a chilly calm settled over him. He would wipe the smug grin off the bastard's face. Stepping back, he slid the short, thin blade in his left hand into a sheath at his waist. Rotating the blade in his right hand, he countered another thrust as he stepped to the side.

"I will get the answers I want and when I am done, you will wish you had been the first one to die instead of your comrades," Ristèard said in a voice devoid of emotion.

"You'll be the one dead, Grand Ruler," the male hissed as he circled to Ristèard's right. "You should have kept both blades, you might have had a chance."

"Who says I didn't," Ristèard murmured with satisfaction.

He swung the weapon in his hand in an arc in front of him. His finger slid over the second button on the handle, releasing dozens of tiny blades tipped with a slow activating poison. The weapon was one of his own inventions and had saved his life many times in the past.

Surprise lit the face of the other male as the deadly missiles pierced his chest, arms, and stomach. Ristèard knew he would have just a short time to extract the information he wanted before the male died. He had learned from his grandfather's murder that it was best to eliminate the threat as quickly as possible. His grandfather had died trying to get information out of one of the men that had come to kill him.

The loud clatter of the sword echoed through the long, dark corridor of the palace. He watched as the man sank down to his knees, his gaze glued to Ristèard's cold silver eyes. The poison was already beginning to paralyze the assassin's muscles.

"I expected you to resist longer," the man whispered hoarsely.

"You expected wrong," Ristèard replied, stepping forward. He tilted his head as he ran the tip of his blade along the man's cheek where the woman had cut him. "Who sent you?"

"I will never... tell... you," the man hissed out.

Ristèard shook his head. "Wrong answer," he said coldly, striking the man and knocking him onto his side on the floor. "I will have the answers to my questions before I let you die."

His eyes flickered to the door that glowed brightly before collapsing inward. Three of his four personal guards, each one carefully selected by him, briefly stood in the entrance surveying the room before stepping inside. Each of them were covered in blood, some of it their own, most of it from whomever they had fought.

They had returned to Elpidios only to discover a trap had been set for them. He expected no less. He knew there were members of the council who thought he was not doing enough to save their world. The fact that the bastards were the reason it was dying was a moot point.

"Ristèard," Andras called as he, Emyr, and Sadao moved cautiously forward.

"Where is Harald?" Ristèard asked, turning his attention back to the dying man beginning to writhe in front of him as the poison slowly moved through his body.

"Playing with his assassin," Emyr replied, glancing at the male on the floor before studying the other two dead assassins. "It looks like there were nine of them this time."

"Find Harald," Ristèard ordered, turning his attention back to his attacker. "I will meet you in my office once I'm done here."

Andras raised his hand and the other two men nodded. A faint smile curved Ristèard's lips. He knew that Andras would not leave him alone again. Bending down, he rolled the writhing figure onto his back.

"Now, you will tell me what you know," he said, raising his blade.

* * *

Two hours later, Ristèard stood looking out the window of his office. The shields were holding over the planet, but barely. Soon, massive evacuations of the cities would be necessary and the secondary shields would have to be activated to protect only them.

The Blood Crystals he had returned with would temporarily help his world, but they needed more, much more, if it was to survive. His species could handle a greater amount of radiation than most, but even they could not survive if the levels increased much more. A knock on his office door drew his attention away from the muted sunlight shining through the tinted windows.

"Enter," he ordered, turning to face the door.

His hand relaxed on the blade at his side when he saw Andras at the door. He nodded and turned back to study the city below him. Life moved on as if there was no concern that it could all end tomorrow.

The image of a delicate face suddenly formed in his mind. The face of a woman with hair the color of the sun, eyes the color of new born babe on Elpidios, and skin the color of the night flowers that only bloomed on the double full moons. Was the prophecy true? Was she the one who would save his world? If so, how? How could a woman, especially an alien from another world, save it when she knew nothing about them?

Andras silently walked across the room to stand next to him. For a moment, neither of them said anything as they looked down on the city. They had brought back a brief reprieve. The crystals the Kassians replicated worked, but they were smaller and weaker than the ones once found in plentiful abundance on the surface of the planet.

Andras sighed heavily before he spoke. "The assassin Harald was after had no new information. All Harald was able to get from the male before he died was that the new leader would emerge on the anniversary of Elpidios Rising, an event that happened only once every two thousand years. It was a time when the third moon moved out of the shadow of its larger siblings and shone full. That is the same thing each of them has said over the past two years," he stated. "I fear we are no closer to finding out who is behind the attacks now, than we were before your father's death. I say we kill all the council members and be done with it."

An amused smile curved Ristèard's lips at Andras' comment. "You are beginning to sound like me," he responded.

"Our world is dying," Andras murmured, staring down at the movement of people far below. "Even with the Kassisan's help, there is no way to produce enough to keep the shields active for any length of time. Already, there are parts of the planet that are becoming uninhabitable. It would be better to start the evacuation."

"And what, seal ourselves below ground so we die a slower death?" Ristèard asked harshly. "No, there is one other option."

Andras looked at Ristèard in surprise. "What option? Do the Kassisans have more crystals they would give us?" He asked with a puzzled frown.

"No, they supposedly have something far more valuable," Ristèard replied, turning away from the window and walking over to his desk.

Andras glared at Ristèard's back in frustration. "What do they have?"

Ristèard pressed a button on the tablet on his desk. The image of a female, the one he had been thinking about earlier, appeared. He stared at the pale alien features, surprised at the instant attraction he felt when he gazed at the vivid blue eyes looking back at him with just a touch of irritation in them. His lips curved upward as he remembered her low, furious words to him a few weeks before.

"The fabled Empress of Elpidios, my mythical bride," Ristèard replied, looking up at Andras' shocked face. "The prophecy states she will save our world. I suggest we put it to the test."

Andras glanced from the holographic image of the woman to Ristèard and back again. His mouth opened and closed twice as he tried to think of how this strange, pale creature was supposed to be the prophesied Empress all young Elpidios' children learned about at bedtime.

Skepticism darkened his features as he stared at his friend and leader. "Do you really believe it? She doesn't even look like us. She is very... pale," he added with a grimace. "Besides, everyone knows the legend is just a tale to give hope to young children."

Ristèard continued to stare at the image, lost in thought. Yes, it was a tale told to give young children hope. Yet, behind all great tales, there is a thread of truth. He thought of one of his commanding officers, Mena Rue, and her passionate insistence that the ancient tablets her parents found spoke of the first sign telling of the coming of the great Empress.

What concerned him was the fact that so far, what had been foretold was actually happening! The battle against the traitorous Kassisan and the three unusual females who had saved the lives of Torak and Jazin Ja Kel Coradon, two of the three ruling members of the House of Kassis, were too much of a coincidence for him to ignore. Not only were there three great warrior women, they had been instrumental in saving the house of Kassis and they had brought back an unusual group of warriors, including a female that looked suspiciously like…

"Instruct Commander Rue that I want to see her immediately," Ristèard suddenly ordered, looking up at Andras. "I also want any information *Dedeis* Rue and his bride have deciphered from the ancient tablets they have found."

Andras bowed his head before he started for the door. He paused as it opened to turn and look at Ristèard with a frown. His eyes moved back to the holographic image.

"How do you propose finding out if she is truly the Empress that will save our world?" Andras asked, quietly. "What if she does not agree to help us?"

Ristèard looked up from the image with a scowl. "She will," he replied arrogantly.

"How do you know?" Andras asked.

"Because she will have no other choice," Ristèard responded with a determined glint in his eye. "She will help us, even if I have to kidnap her to do it."

Andras didn't say anything for a moment before a reluctant grin tugged at his lips. It would appear that things were about to become very interesting… one way or the other. They were either going to discover they had found the prophesied Empress of the Elpidios Rising, or they were going to be at war with the Kassisans. Either way, life for the people of Elpidios, and their Grand Ruler, was about to change.

"I'll instruct Commander Rue to come immediately and bring any information she might have," Andras replied. "And, I'll warn Emyr, Sadao, and Harald to prepare for a covert mission."

Ristèard nodded in agreement. He slowly sank down into the large chair behind his desk, his eyes glued to the image of Ricki Bailey. For a moment, a sense of indecision washed through him. Pushing it aside, he leaned forward and tapped a command into the console on his desk.

A second image, this time from the ancient tablets *Dedeis* Rue had discovered, appeared. He wanted to compare the information Commander Rue brought him with what he had already obtained. For her sake, and the sake of her parents, it had better match or be more in depth than what he currently had on file.

"Who are you?" He whispered, carefully studying the two images. "How can this even be possible?"

The images were almost identical. The color on the stone tablet was faded and a portion of it was missing, but the facial features looked as if Ricki Bailey had posed for the etching on the two thousand year old stone. If there was one thing he did not like, it was unanswered questions.

"Enter," he called when a soft knock sounded at the door.

The slender blue figure of a woman stepped inside, a sultry smile on her face. She was dressed in the traditional gown worn by most women. It wrapped around her figure and folded over one delicate, blue shoulder before being pinned by a large, black broach. He scowled when she closed the door behind her and reached up to unclasp the pin holding the top of her gown.

"I'd heard you had returned," she whispered. "I am here to pleasure you, my lord Grand Ruler."

Chapter 3

Ricki scanned the tent, looking for her father. A smile curved her lips when she saw he was talking with Stan, the computer genius behind many of their shows. Stan was a very nice man and had been trying to get her to go out with him for the past year.

The problem with that was she had a very strict rule about dating members of the circus. She wanted to make sure that anyone she dated was interested in her and not in her father and mother's wealth. It would also make life difficult if things did not work out. Since she had no intentions of leaving the circus, it would mean either living with the person or they would have to leave.

Ricki considered herself a very calm, logical person who looked at all possible scenarios. Based on the probability of such a relationship not working out, she had decided the best avenue to maintain a happy and healthy work and home environment was to avoid any type of personal relationships with those that traveled with them. Since that only left dating those not associated with the circus, which was constantly on the move, it meant that she had not had any relationships to speak of. Oh, she had gone out on the occasional date with someone she had met during their travels, but she quickly found they were more enamored with her lifestyle than with her. That realization often turned into death for any promise of a second date.

Now, well... now, she might have to rethink her strict guidelines since they were no longer on Earth. Her gaze moved around the tent, taking in the familiar faces mixed with not so familiar ones. A light blush rose in her cheeks when she saw one of the Kassisan guards she had grown used to being around looking at her with interest.

No, she thought, schooling her face into the serene mask that she always wore when she felt self-conscious, *things were not the same as they had been before.*

Turning, she smiled at Jo Strauss, or Jo Ja Kel Coradon, as she was now called. Jo was her best friend and the only one who really knew and understood how inadequate Ricki often felt. She wasn't talented like Jo and her younger sister, Star. She couldn't fly through the air, or throw knives like River Knight-Ja Kel Coradon, or write complex programs like Stan, or make people laugh, or the hundreds of other things that her friends and surrogate circus family could do. She was good at two things, organizing things and dealing with the hundreds of complex problems that came with moving a circus the size of Cirque de Magik from one place to the other.

The smile on her face grew as she watched Marvin and Martin, the two Mimes who turned out to be aliens, stop Manota Ja Kel Coradon, Jo's husband. She had always been fascinated by them. They were just so good at what they did that even she often got caught up in their antics. The discovery that they were not human didn't make her think differently about them. If anything, it made them fit in even more. Her father and mother had welcomed such a variety of misfits and lost souls over the years, that they were just part of the norm.

Who am I kidding, Ricki thought with a sigh. *I'm just as much a misfit as the rest. Maybe that is why I never want to leave.*

Her mom and dad had sat down with her when she was five years old and explained how she had come to be a part of their life. By then, she was almost as tall as her mom. She remembered asking her mom why she looked so different from them.

* * *

"Mom, why do I have yellow hair when you and daddy both have brown hair," she remembered asking. "Star and Jo look like their parents, yet I don't look anything like you and dad."

Her mother had looked at her dad for several long seconds before she had gently taken her hand and sat her down. Ricki remembered how her mom had told her about finding her on the steps of their trailer. She had listened carefully, nodding as both of her parents told her that she was a wonderful gift to them and they loved her very, very much.

"Do you think they will come back for me?" She had asked, afraid. "If we keep moving, they won't be able to find me, right? I don't want them to take me away from you and dad."

"Oh, Ricki," Nema had responded, pulling her into her arms and holding her trembling body. "No,

Ricki, we would never let them take you away from us. You are our little girl, isn't that right, Walter? You are ours!"

"Damn right," Walter assured her in a gruff voice. "We are your parents, Ricki. And let me tell you, every single member of this circus would fight to keep you with us, too. You are our little girl forever, no matter what!" He declared, throwing his arms out wide.

"You're damn right, dad," Ricki declared passionately with a stubborn tilt to her chin. "I never want to leave you, mom, or the circus!"

Ricki chuckled softly as she remembered her fierce response. It had taken both her and her parents by surprise, but it had been the moment she knew she would never leave the circus. Every single member accepted her as she was, just plain, ordinary, Ricki. They didn't care that she couldn't do all the wonderful, magical things they could. They just loved her for being her... shy, logical, organized, practical, Ricki.

"Ricki!" Jo called out, snapping her out of her reverie.

"Hi, Jo," Ricki responded, chuckling when she heard a low snarl from Manota as Marvin pulled a long scarf out of his ear. "I hope Manota doesn't kill them."

Jo snorted and glanced over at Manota with a loving gaze. "Are you kidding me? After what those two turned into a few weeks ago? I don't think anything could kill them."

Ricki smiled when Martin turned to look at her. Her gaze softened at his intense, questioning look. It was as if he were trying to see her reaction. She bowed her head slightly to let him know that she was okay with his and Marvin's new status as resident aliens of the circus.

"How is Thea doing?" Ricki asked quietly. "She was very upset. Has she forgiven them yet?"

Jo shook her head. "I don't think so. She isn't saying much, but I don't think finding out the two men that she loves are something much different than she thought is what has her upset. I think it is the fact they didn't tell her that is bothering her the most," she replied with a sigh.

Ricki nodded, watching as the two brothers turned and silently walked out of the huge tent. "I think they are finished teasing your husband," Ricki chuckled.

"I asked them to hold him off if he came after me," Jo admitted with an amused twinkle in her eye. "Ever since he found out I was pregnant, he has been trying to keep me under lock and key. He is terrified of me doing anything."

"Go to him," Ricki murmured with a slightly sad smile. "He only wants to protect you. It is obvious he loves you very deeply."

She watched as Jo turned to look at where Manota stood staring at them, worry and love in his eyes, as he ran them over Jo's slightly rounded figure. She nodded when Jo murmured she would see her later. Something told Ricki that Jo probably would be very occupied. Just thinking about that, brought another faint blush to Ricki's cheeks. She wondered what it would feel like to be loved so totally.

"You are as beautiful as ever, Ricki," Stan commented, walking up to her. "When are you going to give in and let me take you to dinner?"

Ricki turned in surprise. She studied Stan for several long seconds before deciding that she needed to make a decision. She was no longer on Earth. If she was going to have a relationship, wasn't it better to be with someone she knew, trusted, and respected? Stan was all of those things. While he did not make her pulse speed up like…

"How about tonight?" Ricki suddenly responded, jerking her thoughts away from where they were going. "That is if… "

"Tonight is great," Stan immediately agreed with an easy grin. "I'll come by your trailer just before dark. There is this great place in town that I've found."

Ricki tilted her head in agreement and pushed her glasses up. "That sounds lovely," she said with a nervous smile. "I look forward to seeing you later this evening. If you'll excuse me, I have a few things to discuss with my father. Until later."

Ricki nodded and gave Stan a shy smile watching as he turned and walked over to where one of the clowns was working on some of the rigging and needed some help. She refused to acknowledge the flutter in her stomach. It was past time that she made a decision on what she wanted to do with her life.

Stan had proven he was dependable, nice, caring, and now it didn't matter about her parents' wealth, she highly doubted Earth currency was accepted here.

"Dad, I need to talk to you about a few things if you have a moment," Ricki called, turning back to her father.

* * *

Walter glanced at Ricki and felt a wave of pride and worry before he turned his attention back to Marcus. The 'Magician Extraordinaire' was really a master pickpocket and street hustler who had learned his trade on the streets of Las Vegas. He was just one of dozens of people that had gravitated to the circus looking for a way of life that both protected them from their past and gave them the rush they needed.

"I'll be right there, Ricki," Walter responded with a nod. "Marcus, work with Stan to check how everyone is doing tomorrow. This is still new to everyone and I know that some of the scientists are coming tomorrow to check the animals we have."

Marcus grimaced. "You know how protective Katarina is about her cats, Walter," he groaned. "She is just as likely to tell them to eat the aliens than allow any of them near one of her babies."

"Well, make sure she doesn't," Walter grunted as he turned away. "Tell her to keep those damn cats under control, that eating our hosts won't help them accept us."

"Damn it," Marcus grumbled, turning away. "I hate dealing with that crazy Russian. She always sends one of those damn cats after my ass."

"Yeah, well, she wouldn't have if she hadn't caught you trying to stuff the ocelot cub in one of your magical disappearing boxes," Stan observed, wiping his hands from where he was helping one of the clowns with some equipment. "I warned you she was protective of them."

Walter shook his head as the two men walked out of the tent. Marcus was right, Katarina Danshov was extremely picky about her assortment of feline companions, to the point she was never without one or more of them by her side. He didn't question how she kept them under control. Now that he knew aliens actually existed, he decided that it wasn't so strange after all.

"What do you need, love?" Walter asked, looking up at her. "I swear you grow more beautiful each day. When are you going to find you a young man? You know your mom is itching to have a grand baby."

Ricki rolled her eyes and pressed her lips together to keep the groan from escaping. Now that River, Star, and Jo were expecting, her mom had been dropping hints about how she would love to have a grandson or granddaughter to cuddle with.

She just kept pointing out that in order to have a baby that it helped to have a husband first. That led to her mom posting a long list of eligible men on her tablet this morning. Shaking her head at her dad, she stared down at the tablet in her hand instead.

"You are just as bad as mom," Ricki grumbled under her breath.

Walter huffed and folded his arms across his chest. "We aren't getting any younger and neither are you," he stated before his gaze softened on her flushed cheeks. "We just don't want you to be alone, Ricki. If something should happen to your mom and I..."

Ricki's gaze quickly focused on her dad's face. Concern and fear darkened her vivid blue eyes as she stared down at him. For a moment, she bit her lip in worry. Was either one of them sick? She could schedule an appointment with the healers here. The medical staff seemed much more sophisticated than back on Earth. Surely if something was wrong, the doctors here could cure it.

"Are you or mom sick?" Ricki asked in a husky tone. "I can schedule an appointment with Shavic immediately. River says he is wonderful."

Walter's arms fell to his side before he reached over and gripped Ricki's hand in reassurance. Shaking his head, he led her over to the aluminum stands and waited for her to sit down. Nema had asked him to have a talk with Ricki.

"Uh, Ricki, I've been meaning to discuss something with you," Walter began in an uncomfortable voice as he paced slightly back and forth in front of where she was sitting. "Your mom and I... well... She thought it might be better if I talked to you about this, to give you a little of a man's point of view and all."

* * *

Ricki's eyes widened before she lowered her eyelids to hide the amusement and mortification in them. Something told her she wasn't going to like what her father had to say. Her eyes flickered up to his face again when he cleared his throat.

"Now, Ricki," he started out gruffly. "There are some things in life that happen naturally. Take for example, a man meeting a woman or vice-versa. When a man finds a woman attractive, he will show it in many different ways. If he knows what is good for him, he'll do the right thing and come ask me for permission to court you."

Ricki watched her dad with rounded eyes when he suddenly stopped in front of her and glowered at her with a fierceness that had sunk men four times his height. She had discovered it wasn't height that made a man, but the way he carried himself. Her dad was taller and fiercer than any of the alien warriors… even the big blue one, in her personal opinion.

"And if he doesn't?" Ricki asked in curiosity, tilting her head to look at her dad. "What then?"

"I'll roast his balls over an open flame and feed the rest of his ass to Katarina's tigers," her dad growled in a low, fierce tone. "If the man respects you, he'll come ask me first. If he doesn't, he isn't worth Tony's elephant piss, if you ask me."

Ricki blinked several times before she bit her lip and looked toward the opening of the tent. "I… Stan," she started to say before looking back at her dad.

"Stan already asked me if he could court you," Walter replied with a sigh. "He has been bugging the hell out of me for over a year now."

"Dad, you don't think that maybe, courting might be a little old fashioned, do you? I mean, I am twenty-four," Ricki replied in a gentle, soothing tone. "I'm old enough to make my own decisions."

She set the tablet that she was holding down on her lap when her dad reached his hands out to her. Grasping his smaller, thicker fingers with her long, slender ones, she felt his reassuring squeeze. Her face softened with love when she saw how worried he really was about her.

"You may be twenty-four, Ricki, but you'll always be my little girl," he said. "I'm an old-fashioned father, if you haven't noticed. I promised your mother's parents the day I asked for her hand in marriage that I would always protect her. I made that same promise to your mother when she found you. Personally, I don't think any man is good enough for you, but if I had to choose one, Stan would almost be. He can be a goof-ball sometimes, but his heart is in the right place."

Ricki looked down at their entwined fingers. She didn't want him to see the hint of doubt and worry in her eyes. She knew Stan was a nice guy. The problem was, he didn't make her heart race or her body heat up. Only one man had done that recently and it had been because she was angry enough to throttle him. It wasn't often that she got annoyed at someone, but there was something about Ristèard Roald that had rubbed her the wrong way.

She thought back to almost a month ago. The first time she became aware of Ristèard Roald was when she caught a glimpse of him standing inside the entrance to the main tent. He had almost attacked Marvin and Martin. Now that she knew what the two Mimes could do, she almost wished her dad hadn't interfered.

Still, it had been rather entertaining watching her dad as he lit into him. The expression on the man's face had been priceless. He looked like he wasn't sure what to do as confusion twisted his face as he stared down at her dad.

While he was extremely good looking for someone that looked like they had been dunked into a toilet tank filled with blue cleaning tablets, he was far too arrogant for her. She had met enough diplomats like him to last her a lifetime! It had only taken a glance at his stiff, broad shoulders and ruggedly handsome face, not to mention half the women and one or two of the men in the tent drooling, to let her know he was all too aware of his own importance.

The second time she saw Ristèard Roald had been the night that a horrible battle occurred. Ricki had been terrified, not so much for herself, but for her mom, dad, and her other circus family who had volunteered to help stop a horrible man, a Kassisan traitor, who had almost killed River, Jo, and Star. He had shown up for their first performance with more than a dozen mercenaries.

The fact that it was a trap to catch the man didn't matter to Ricki. All she knew was that someone she loved might die that night. Stan had been concerned about her and had stopped her outside the entrance shortly before the performance. He had also wanted her to go out with him when it was over. Shortly after that, Ristèard had stopped her, demanding to know who Stan was and why he was touching her.

She had coolly dismissed his question, but he had gripped her hand, preventing her from completing her assigned task. If that hadn't been bad enough, he had added an additional insult. Even now, she could feel her skin tingle from where he had held her hand and his intense, possessive gaze was burned into her memory.

"Good, I am claiming you as mine. You may go for now," he had arrogantly said.

Ricki's cheeks flamed as she remembered his haughty attitude. She never used profanity, but that night, she had on more than one occasion. It was what happened after the battle that sealed her intense dislike and determination to stay away from the man.

"Ricki, are you okay?" Her dad asked, bringing her back to the present. "You look a little flushed. Maybe you should see one of those doctors, or get Tank to take a look at you."

Ricki blinked and squeezed her dad's hands before letting them go. Picking up the tablet, she rose gracefully off the metal bench. She drew in a deep breath and smiled down at her dad.

"I'm fine," she promised. "I just wanted to go over a few things with you."

"So, you agree about Stan?" Walter asked with a pleased smile.

Ricki schooled her face to hide her confusion. She didn't have a clue about what her dad had been saying the last few minutes. Giving him a non-committal smile, she changed the subject.

"Stan and I are going out tonight," she replied, grasping the tablet firmly in her hands. "Now, I really need to talk to you about ordering the items on this list. From the research I've done and the discussions I've had with Tony, Katarina and the others, they agree the food supplements should work if we gradually incorporate them into the animals' diets."

Ricki breathed a silent sigh of relief when her dad dropped her love life and focused back on the circus. She wondered if this is why most girls moved out. She would have to ask Jo about it later.

Chapter 4

"Do you have her in sight?" Ristèard growled into the comlink as he landed his air skid on the top of a nearby roof.

"Yes," Harald replied. "They are sitting on the outside patio near the water."

"I will be there shortly," Ristèard snapped as fury poured through him. "If they leave, whatever happens, don't lose them."

"What if this alien male has already claimed her?" Andras asked quietly, shutting off his own air skid and stepping up next to Ristèard. "It has been a month since you left. If you have not shown your intention to claim her, she may have accepted another."

Ristèard glared over his shoulder at Andras before he turned his attention back to where he was going. Night had fallen over the city, making it easier to move under the cover of its inky darkness. The moons would not rise for another hour.

Grasping the side of the building, he gauged the distance to the top of the building next door from one they landed on. He stepped back, ignoring Andras' statement. It wouldn't matter what the alien female decided, he had already told her that she belonged to him. When he made up his mind, he seldom changed it. He definitely had no intentions of altering it about this female.

Sprinting forward, he jumped on the low wall and catapulted himself to the roof below landing and rolling before standing up and moving to the edge of it. He heard Andras' low curse drift through the air before his friend and security chief landed beside him.

"You know, we could have just landed closer," Andras grumbled as he dusted himself off. "Might I also point out again that taking a female, especially one under the protection of the royal house, is not a good idea?"

Ristèard shrugged as he leaned over the edge of the roof to stare down at the open patio area of the dining establishment. His eyes were immediately drawn to the female with hair the color of the sun. She was sitting facing in his direction at a table near the water.

His fingers curled around the hard surface of the wall. She was even more beautiful than he remembered; a feat he didn't believe was possible. Hot, molten rage swept through him when the male said something that caused her to laugh. It wasn't the fact that she was laughing that angered him, but the way the male leaned forward and brushed a strand of her hair that had come loose in the light breeze back from her face.

"You're growling," Andras pointed out dryly as he studied the couple below them. "She is very unusual and I have to admit, she does look like the image of the Empress."

Ristèard gritted his teeth to keep from roaring out and attacking the male when he leaned forward and brushed a light kiss on Ricki's cheek as they stood up to leave. He studied the male. It was the same one from the night in front of the tent. He would recognize the male's shaggy brown hair and lean frame anywhere. As far as he was concerned, the male was a dead man.

"Let's go," he ordered, turning and striding to the outer steps that led down off the terrace balcony. "I want the female."

Andras eyed the woman who stood next to the alien male. With a shake of his head, he still couldn't believe how an alien female was supposed to save his planet. Turning, he quickly followed Ristèard down the steps.

* * *

Ricki smiled at Stan and murmured her thanks as he held out her yellow sweater. She was wearing a light, sleeveless matching yellow dress that came to just above her knees and a pair of matching flat, dress shoes. She found when she wore heels that she often towered over the men she dated. While Stan was the same height as her, if she had worn the heels she had slipped on earlier, she would have been an inch taller than him.

At almost six feet three inches, she had learned to accept her unusual height. Still, it was nice feeling more feminine and delicate when she was with a man. She raised her face to the breeze and looked around her.

"It is beautiful here," she admitted with a slight laugh." If I didn't know better, I'd think that we were back on Earth."

Stan's chuckle blended with hers. "Yeah, if you can get past the glowing crystals, the purple water, and the fact that we'll be staring up at twin moons, it is just a walk through Paris," he teased, sliding his arm around her. "There is a boardwalk that runs along the river that I thought you might enjoy."

Ricki nodded. "That sounds very nice," she said, stepping around the tables. "How did you find this place?"

"I asked River and Star," Stan admitted. "Then, came and checked it out a couple of days ago."

Ricki gazed around as they stepped back into the street. Thin pillars stood every ten feet along the busy roadway. They glittered with a bright light that caught and shone a soft light for the pedestrians milling about the open store fronts. Transports with no tires slid past them with just enough of a purr to warn those crossing to beware. Even the sidewalks lit up as they stepped on them.

"It all seems so magical," Ricki commented as Stan guided her around several people who slowed to stare at them. "I'm not used to being stared at so much," she admitted with a shy, self-conscious laugh.

"Neither am I," Stan admitted with an easy grin. "We're usually behind the scenes. Come on," he muttered, sliding his arm from around her waist so he could grab her hand. "I don't know about you, but I'm tired of being the main attraction."

Ricki laughed when he suddenly began to jog slowly away from the growing crowd. They were both breathless and laughing when he finally slowed down as they passed through the gates of a riverside park. She pulled away and stepped closer to a nearby bench that was in the shadows of a large tree. Setting her silver purse down on the bench, she reached up to redo her long hair back into the bun she normally wore.

"Don't," Stan suddenly said in a husky voice. "I don't think I've ever seen you with your hair down."

Ricki paused, startled. A delicate frown creased her brow. For a moment, indecision swept through her. She really had enjoyed her evening, and while the evening had been almost magical, it was more due to the location than to the handsome man standing in front of her.

"Stan," Ricki started to say before her voice faded.

Stan reached up and gently pulled her hand away. The long, golden strands shimmered in the faint light cast by the glowing pillars. Ricki heard his breath catch in a gasp when he saw how long and thick it was.

Her hair was one of her most treasured assets. She was very self-conscious of her size eleven shoes and size B cup breasts. Her eyes were not an amazing dark blue like River's, but an icy blue that was very useful in keeping uncooperative officials in line. She had perfected a certain look over the years that could freeze an argument within seconds.

The one thing she did love about her appearance was her hair. It glittered with a sheen that caught the smallest fragment of light and made it almost glow. It was so blonde, that at times, it looked as if it was blended with the white threads of a snowflake the way it glittered in the light.

"It is beautiful," he whispered, threading his fingers through it even as he stepped closer. "Just like you, Ricki."

Ricki's lips parted in surprise when he suddenly slid his other arm around her waist and pulled her close. Her hands rose on their own to slide between them, spreading across his chest to instinctively stop him, before she forced them to relax. She wanted, needed to know, if there was any spark between them.

Her eyelids fluttered closed as he pressed his lips to hers in a slow, sensual kiss. She analyzed the kiss, noting the warmth and firmness of his lips, the slight pressure on her lower back and in her hair, and the way he tilted his head. He tasted like the hot drink they had sampled that was similar to the coffee she enjoyed in the mornings. It wasn't unpleasant. In fact, the kiss was probably, on a scale of zero to ten, about a seven or eight, she decided as he pulled back.

Her eyelashes fluttered before rising to look at him in curiosity. Silver eyes, touched with a hint of exasperation combined with amusement, glittered back at her. Her lips parted as she drew in a deep breath.

"I swear I could hear your mind working," Stan observed with a hint of dry amusement in his voice. "Would you be interested in sharing your deep thoughts?"

Ricki blushed, but didn't look away from him. Tilting her head to the side, a smile curved her lips before a low chuckle escaped her and she shook her head. She started to lower her head, but stopped when he caught her chin in the hand that had been in her hair and tilted her head back.

"Tell me," he insisted.

Ricki bit her bottom lip and looked at him in indecision. "You aren't going to like my answer," she cautioned.

Stan gave her a lopsided grin. "I'm a big boy. I think I can handle it," he assured her.

"I was analyzing your kiss," she explained. "It was very interesting."

Stan's eyes widened at her surprising statement. A low chuckle escaped him again and he shook his head. Ricki could see he was fighting his curiosity to know what conclusion she'd come or whether he was better off not knowing.

"Okay," he laughed. "I think this is a first, but go ahead. I'm fascinated to discover your findings."

"That will not be necessary," a menacing voice snarled out of the darkness.

Ricki gasped as the familiar form of Ristèard Roald stepped out of the shadows of the tree near them. She took a startled step back when the light from the nearby pillar briefly washed across his face. He looked furious!

"Hey, I know you," Stan commented with a frown. "You're that Grand Ruler or something from Elope-something or other, aren't you?"

"Elpidios," Ricki automatically corrected as Ristèard stepped closer to them. She eyed him warily. "Grand Ruler," she greeted in an icy tone.

"Take your hands off her," Ristèard demanded, his eyes glued to Ricki's face.

Stan instinctively did the opposite. His right arm slid around Ricki's waist, pulling her protectively closer to his body. Ricki saw the confused frown darken his face as he tried to understand what was going on. She was just as confused.

"Sir, there is no need to trouble yourself," Ricki explained in a soothing tone. "Stan and I are having an enjoyable evening out together. If you don't mind, I'd like to continue it without interruption."

Ricki knew immediately that she had said something wrong, though she couldn't think what it could have been. She replayed her statement in her head, turning it over to see if there could have been anything offensive in it, and drew a blank.

"Take him out," Ristèard ordered as two other men appeared out of the darkness behind him.

"Take me…," Stan repeated at the same time as Ricki did.

"Take him… Now, wait just one minute," she exclaimed, trying to step in front of Stan. A loud gasp escaped her when a pair of strong hands wrapped around her waist and lifted her up against his body. "I... Oh, what do you think you are doing?!"

Ricki frantically pushed against the broad, muscular shoulders. Her head turned quickly when she heard the sound of scuffling behind her. Panic erupted through her when she saw Stan strike out at one of the men.

"Stan!" She cried out, struggling to get free.

"Run, Ricki," Stan yelled to her before he grunted as the second man grabbed his arm and hit him in the stomach.

Ricki's head swiveled back to look down in fury. Raising her right hand, she started to swing it in an effort to strike Ristèard across the face. A low cry escaped her and her hand fell back to his shoulder when she felt her body sliding down his until her feet touched the ground. His hand swept up to grasp her wrist when she started to swing again.

"I don't think so," he growled in a low tone.

Ricki's eyes flashed in vehemence when she saw the amusement in his eyes. He thought attacking them was funny? He thought she was some delicate little flower that couldn't defend herself? Well, she had learned a thing or two over the years from her circus family and one of them was to never give up.

Pulling unsuccessfully on her wrist in an attempt to break free, she reacted instinctively, raising her knee at the same time as she used her nails to pinch his ear with her free hand. A grimace escaped her when she felt her knee connect with the soft flesh of his balls. She refused to feel any sympathy for the sudden flash of surprise, followed by intense pain that entered his eyes. If she hadn't been so tall, it would have been impossible for her to have used that maneuver on him.

Triumph filled her when he bent forward and braced his hands on his knees in an effort to remain standing. His shuddering breaths were a testament that she had struck him hard. Taking advantage of his vulnerability, she pulled back and popped him on the tip of his nose just like Marvin had taught her. She remembered that Martin always told her to hit her attacker while they were still disoriented. The double assault sent Ristèard backwards onto his ass along the soft grassy surface that edged the walkway.

Turning away, she saw Stan striking out at one of the men attacking him. She focused on the man closest to her that was trying to circle back around behind Stan. The moment the man turned his back to her, she kicked out her leg. Her foot connected with his backside sending him headfirst into the other man when Stan suddenly twisted.

"Run!" She cried out, reaching for Stan when he jerked backwards out of the way of the two men.

Stan turned toward her and reached for her outstretched hand before he jerked and froze. His eyes widened and his mouth opened and closed several times before they rolled back in his head and he collapsed. A low cry of terror escaped Ricki when she saw a fourth man step out of the darkness holding some type of weapon. Turning, she fled.

Chapter 5

Emyr bent and held his hand out to Ristèard who was lying on his back, still drawing in deep breaths as wave after wave of pain radiated through him. He could care less about his nose. He'd had that broken more than once in the past. No, it was his balls that he was worried about. He had never been hit in that sensitive spot before and hoped to the Goddess that he never would be again.

"Don't... lose her," he bit out between gritted teeth.

Emyr gave Ristèard a sympathetic nod before he closed his hand around his friend's. "Sadao is following her," he responded. "She won't get far."

Ristèard emitted a low curse as he forced himself into a standing position. Wiping the back of his hand under his nose, he ignored the blood on the back of it. It wasn't broken, but it hurt like hell. Shrugging Emyr's hand off his shoulder, he looked at the other three men.

"Sadao, where is she?" He asked into the comlink.

The sound of heavy breathing surprised him. He would have thought Sadao would have caught Ricki by now, unless she used the same defense on the guard as she did on him. He was about to demand Sadao's location again when his guard replied.

"She has disappeared," Sadao responded in frustration. "I know she is close by, though."

Ristèard bit back the curse threatening to escape him. His eyes moved to the sky and the faint glow of the first moon rise. Before long, it would be more difficult to keep their position undisclosed. Turning, he nodded to Emyr and Harald.

"You two get the air-skids and meet us at Sadao's location. We are going to have to leave in a hurry. Once Ajaska or Torak find out we are here, they are going to want to know why," Ristèard said sharply. "Let's go."

He didn't wait for the others. A slight groan escaped him when he felt his balls shift against the material of his pants as he ran. He had fought several women over the course of his life, most trained assassins, but never had any of them been as successful at putting him on his ass as Ricki had been.

A reluctant admiration for her rose up inside of him. She had not only put him on the ground, but two of his best warriors. Of course, they had greatly underestimated her, something that would not happen again.

He was surprised at the distance it took before he and Andras caught up with Sadao. The warrior was carefully walking through a small wooded area.

Ristèard nodded when Sadao turned to him in frustration. He was surprised when he saw the line of fresh blood along Sadao's temple. Coming to a stop in front of his friend, he glanced around with a frown.

"Where is she?" Ristèard demanded before his brow creased even further. "And what the hell happened to you?"

Sadao gave a nod to Andras. "She is somewhere in this wooded area, and she is what happened to me. There was a low limb along the path I didn't see. She pulled it back and let it go just as I was about to catch her. It knocked me on my ass. She is fast, Ristèard. I swear I have never seen a woman run as fast as she can."

"Are you sure she is there?" Ristèard asked, looking into the small clump of trees.

Sadao nodded. "I could see all the way through them. There is no way I could have missed her. She went in, but never came out."

Ristèard studied the wooded area carefully before he nodded to the other two men. With a wave of his hand, they split up. He took the center, while Andras took the left and Sadao took the right.

Stepping onto the dark path that cut through the thin grouping of trees, he listened intently as he scanned the path. He paused when he caught a glimpse of pale yellow under a bush. Bending, he picked up a slender shoe. Looking around, he tried to see if he could find any other clues as to where she could have gone.

He paused when he saw another piece of yellow. This time it was her sweater caught on a branch. He glanced around, puzzled, before his gaze rose upwards. He would have missed her hiding among the branches if not for the light breeze that suddenly blew her dress outward.

A grin curved his lips before he pressed them together and emitted a low whistle. It didn't take long for Sadao and Andras to join him. With a nod, he pointed her out to the other two men. She was hiding about ten feet off the ground on a low branch. He could tell she was trying to remain as still and quiet as possible.

Pushing through the bushes, he stepped up under the tree. "I see you, golden hair," he called up to her in a quiet, husky voice. "Come down."

For a moment, she remained frozen, pretending she hadn't heard him before she slowly turned her head and glared down at him. Even from this distance, he could see the stubborn thrust of her jaw. He reached up and rubbed at his chest when a strange tightness pressed against it. She looked so damn beautiful with her bright yellow dress blowing around her. She gripped the tree with one arm while she reached up with the other to impatiently push her long, tangled hair away from her face.

"No," she hissed, wrapping her arm back around the thin trunk of the tree. "Go away! I swear I'm going to scream so loud if you don't... that... that every member of the circus will be able to hear me from here."

"Don't," Ristèard warned sharply. "I mean you no harm. Come down and I will explain."

He released a low growl of frustration when she shook her head again. Holding out her shoe, he muttered for Andras and Sadao to find the other one. He needn't have bothered because the moment he gripped the lower branch of the tree, it hit him on the top of his head with a loud thump.

Stumbling backwards, he would have fallen again if Andras hadn't reached out and grabbed him. He glared up at her, rubbing his now aching head. His heated gaze quickly turned to both Andras and Sadao when they chuckled. He turned back in time to see why. Ricki was now sticking her tongue out at him in defiance.

Andras shrugged when Ristèard glanced back at him with a pained expression. "You've got to admit, she has a good arm," he said, completely unashamed of his amusement.

"And great legs," Sadao added, grinning up at her.

Ristèard punched Sadao in the jaw, knocking him backwards a few steps. "Quit trying to look up her dress," he snapped.

Andras chuckled and stepped back with his hands in the air. "I didn't say anything about her long legs, or about the pretty yellow lace under it."

Ristèard turned when he heard Ricki's outraged gasp. His heart skipped a beat when she let go of the tree and frantically tried to catch her dress that was blowing in the breeze. She wobbled for a moment and almost fell before her left arm caught the trunk again and she pressed herself against it.

"Come down before you fall," he ordered, staring up at her.

She shook her head and pressed her cheek against the smooth bark. Making a decision, Ristèard gripped the limb above his head again and began climbing. It didn't take him long to get to the same branch she was on. Stepping around her, he wrapped his arm tightly around her waist.

"Release the tree, Ricki," he whispered in her ear as he pressed his body against hers.

It took less than a second for him to realize that she was not only trembling violently, but that she was drawing in quick, tiny breaths of air. He could feel the terror running through her body and see the death grip she had on the tree. Steadying himself, he reached up to peel her arm away from the smooth surface.

"Don't!" She whispered frantically, looking at him in panic. "I'm not... Just leave me. Please, just leave me alone."

Ristèard tightened his grip around Ricki's waist, sliding his hand down her arm until he could thread his fingers through hers. He almost winced when she tightened her fingers around his in a surprisingly strong clasp. He muttered under his breath when she didn't let go of the trunk with her other arm.

"Ricki," he started to say, pausing when she shook her head frantically from side to side.

"I can't," she whispered in a tearful voice. "I can't."

Ristèard wondered for a moment if he had made a huge mistake in planning this entire mission. He knew that Ajaska and Torak would never have understood his belief that Ricki was the mythical Empress sent by the Goddess to save his world. Hell, he didn't believe it, but he was desperate.

He needed to return to his world before his absence was noticed. Already, he had been gone too long in his previous negotiation with the Kassisan Royal family. His absence had enabled the traitorous bastards on the council to set a trap for him and his guards. He was scheduled to meet with them tomorrow afternoon. That meant he needed to leave Kassis as soon as possible if he was to return before they noticed he was missing again.

"I swear I will not harm you and neither will my men," he reassured her, wrapping their joined hands around her waist so he could pull her other arm free.

Ricki glanced over her shoulder at him and scowled. "You hurt Stan," she snapped. "How on Earth do you expect me to believe you won't hurt me too? You... What do you want with me anyway?"

Ristèard used her distraction to pull her other arm from the tree. Her loud cry and suddenly stiff body almost toppled them both. It took him a moment to regain his balance on the thin branch. He pulled her close and braced his hand on the trunk of the tree as she dug her nails into his arm.

"Calm or you will make us fall," he ordered, glancing down when Andras called up in a low voice that Harald and Emyr had arrived.

"Oh, God, please don't," Ricki muttered in a terrified voice. "Oh, please don't, please don't, please don't."

Ristèard gritted his teeth in pain. He was sure that he was going to end up with a bloody arm on top of everything else. He shifted his weight until he was balanced and called down to Andras and Sadao.

"I'm sorry, Ricki, but we have to leave now," Ristèard said when the sound of alarms echoed from the direction they had come earlier. The human male's body had been discovered.

Ricki gasped loudly before a loud, piercing scream escaped her as she felt herself falling through the air. Ristèard cursed, knowing that the authorities would hear her. Time was running out and he had done the only thing he could think of to get her out of the tree. He had picked her up and dropped her down to Andras, who was waiting below.

Turning, he jumped, landing on the ground next to where Andras stood holding Ricki in his arms. Taking her shoes from Sadao, he stepped forward and slid them on her bare feet. When he was done, Andras lowered Ricki to the ground.

"Get the...," Ristèard started to order before his head exploded back and he swore he saw the stars up close and personal. "What in the name of the Goddess did you do that for?" He hissed out, holding his now aching jaw.

"You ass!" Ricki hissed in fury, pushing her hair out of her eyes. "You arrogant, horrible excuse for a piece of blue toilet bowl cleaner! I'm *terrified* of heights and you threw me out of a tree! You are the most horrible, terrible... *meanest* person I have ever met!"

Ristèard backed up a step when Ricki swung her fist at him again. He caught it, twisting her around so he could pull her back against his body. A low groan escaped him when she stomped her foot down on his instep in an attempt to break free of his tight embrace.

"Ristèard, we need to leave," Harald warned, glancing down at a scanner. "I have movement headed this way."

Ristèard nodded. With a wave of regret, he knew he was about to make his new, very unwilling Empress even more furious with him. He glanced at Emyr and nodded. Tightening his hold on Ricki as she continued to struggle, he watched as Emyr pressed an injector containing the same drug they used to knock the alien male out against Ricki's neck.

She stiffened and cried out in surprise and shock before he felt her body began to melt against his. Bending, he slid his arm under her knees and straightened, cradling her against his body. With another nod, the small group moved quickly to the air-skids on the other side of the wooded area.

Ristèard adjusted Ricki securely against his body before he started the transport. Lifting upward, he thought it was just as well he had ordered her to be sedated as they rose above the tree line. She would not have enjoyed this part of their journey.

Chapter 6

Ristèard looked up from the report he was studying when the door to his cabin slid open. Andras looked around with a raised eyebrow before returning his eyes to where Ristèard sat on the long couch. They would be landing on Elpidios within the next hour.

There had been a few tense moments on Kassis. Swarms of the security personnel had converged on the area, forcing them to take a longer detour through the city to the transport they had hidden on the outskirts of it. Two of his private security force members had the smaller ship ready for takeoff by the time they arrived.

Harald and Sadao had been working on a new defense system to conceal them from the Kassisan's radars. It had worked well-enough as the local ground control systems registered the ship as a short-range freighter scheduled for a routine run and not an Elpidios star transport. Within an hour of leaving Kassis, they had rendezvoused with his warship, the Elpidios Star.

Once on board, he had ordered Andras to get them back to Elpidios as soon as possible while he carried Ricki's unconscious body to his cabin. He had been surprised by the rush of possessiveness and feelings of jealousy that had coursed through him as he carried her through the long, narrow corridors of the warship. More than one warrior on board had stopped to stare at her long, silky yellow hair that fell in shimmering waves. A dark scowl creased his face as he thought of it.

Since when in the name of the Goddess did he think in terms of shimmering waves? He thought in disgust, glaring at Andras.

"What did I do this time?" Andras asked warily. "You normally only look at me like that when you are ready to kick my ass for some reason."

Ristèard's eyes shifted uneasily to the bed in the corner where Ricki lay sleeping. He needed to get these annoying feelings under control. Frustration and irritation ate at him the more he thought about it.

What was it about her that was getting under his skin? He could appreciate she was unusual and extremely attractive in an exotic way, but he had seen and been with numerous attractive women. He had been fascinated by Jazin Ja Kel Coradon's yellow-haired mate the first time he saw her hair, but he hadn't experienced any of the other emotions beyond curiosity.

Releasing a heavy sigh, Ristèard shook his head. "It is not you," he responded with a wave of his hand toward the chair across from him. "Is there any indication the council is aware of my absence?" He asked, setting the tablet down on the couch next to him.

Andras shook his head. "No, our spies within the council said they are too busy arguing with each other and how they are going to overthrow you to realize that you were gone," Andras said in disgust. "I still think we should just kill them all and be done with it."

Ristèard grimaced. "Not yet. There is at least one of them supporting me. I want to find out who it is and why first," he said, sitting forward with a weary sigh. "The reports are not good, Andras. I will have to make a decision within a matter of weeks about evacuating the planet."

Andras didn't respond, but Ristèard could see the shock on his friend's face. No one, but he and the few select scientists chosen by him, knew just how bad the shields were or the extremely low resources they had left, even with the tons of replicated material coming from Kassis there was little hope.

The Kassisan crystals, while similar, did not react to the radiation the same way the crystals on Elpidios did. No one knew exactly why, but knowing wouldn't change the facts, that without the Blood Crystals, his world would be lost. Yes, the crystals absorbed some of the particle emissions and helped power the generators, but the shields were only a temporary solution. One strategic attack against them and all would be lost. Millions of his people would die from radiation poisoning, not to mention the damage to the environment.

"What of the underground cities?" Andras asked in a quiet voice. "Surely, they could be used. Our ancestors lived there for centuries."

"There are only a handful of them at most that have been found. The last known underground city is where the tablets were discovered. I talked with Mena

Rue's parents who discovered it in the Eastern desert region," Ristèard said grimly with a shake of his head. "The population of our world was much lower centuries ago. The human female is the last hope for our world, Andras. How?… I do not know. I just know that unless a miracle occurs within the next month, or two, millions of our people will die and we will be without a home."

* * *

Ricki lay motionless, listening as the two men talked in a quiet voice. She had been awake for several minutes, trying to figure out where she was and her best plan of attack. Now, listening to them, she began to see things from a different point of view.

She had no doubt they were telling the truth. She had picked up enough information back on Kassis to know why Ristèard Roald was there, she just didn't realize it was so dire. There was something about what they were saying that bothered her, though.

Focusing, she picked up words that were vaguely familiar to her. She remembered reading something similar to what they were talking about in some of the archives back on Kassis when she was researching their history. In fact, she had copied all the files onto a storage chip right before Stan arrived to pick her up and had placed it in her purse to look at later.

It took a moment for her to realize that the other man, Andras, had risen and was leaving. He reminded Ristèard that they would be arriving on Elpidios shortly. She swallowed when she heard the door open and close. For a second, she thought both of the men might have left, but the soft sound of footsteps soon dispelled that hope.

Slowly opening her eyes, she warily watched as Ristèard Roald approached the bed. Sitting up, she pushed her hair out of her eyes and scooted upward when she realized he wasn't going to stop. Her eyes widened in alarm and she leaned backwards when he suddenly knelt on the bed, placing his hands on either side of her.

"You kneed me," he stated in a low, menacing voice. "You hit me."

"Well, you attacked Stan and I first," Ricki retorted softly, pushing the words past her dry throat. "And you *threw* me out of a tree! I'll do even worse if you ever try anything like that again!"

"You called me names," Ristèard added, leaning closer.

Ricki leaned back as far as she could before the wall stopped her. Placing her trembling, right hand on his shoulder, she used her left hand to tuck her messy hair behind her ear. This is why she never wore it down except at night when she was alone.

"I'm sure it was nothing compared to what others have called you in the past," she declared with an icy glare. "Now, if you don't want to have a repeat performance of how I can defend myself, I suggest you get out of my personal space."

She didn't like the way his eyes suddenly narrowed at her threat. Perhaps, she should have used a more diplomatic approach to the situation, but in all honesty, the man *was* in her space and getting closer by the second. She swallowed nervously as she waited to see what he would do next.

Surprise held her when she heard the sound of a dry, rusty chuckle escape him. She thought for a moment that perhaps she might get off relatively easy if he thought what she said was funny. That thought quickly dissolved into confusion when he lifted one hand and wrapped it around the nape of her neck, pulling her forward.

"I want you," he stated before he captured her lips.

Ricki froze in uncertainty. She was being kissed… by the Grand Ruler of Elpidios. Her mind swirled with confusion. She was unsure of what she should do to stop him. She felt her right hand, which had been pressing against his shoulder in a feeble attempt keep space between them, curl against the warm material of his shirt.

A part of her brain was telling her to uncurl and push, not curl and hold as he pressed his lips more firmly over hers. Her lips instinctively parted when she felt the tip of his tongue against them.

A fierce, hot wave of pleasure shot through her, startling her when she felt her nipples pebble and strain against the thin material of her bra. What startled her the most was the liquid heat that pooled low between her legs, making her jerk her knee up in surprise.

She felt Ristèard's body stiffen before a low groan escaped him and he pulled away, rolling onto his side on the bed. Ricki quickly pulled her leg out from under him as he fell sideways. A frown creased her brow as she stared down at his face. His eyes were closed and he was breathing in deeply as if he was in intense pain.

"What...," she started to say when he opened his eyes and glared at her with accusing eyes. Her voice faded when she saw where his hands were. A deep blush rose up to flame her cheeks a bright red. "Oh, sorry."

* * *

Ristèard drew in another deep breath before he even attempted to reply. Her knee had connected perfectly with his crotch again. It hadn't been as hard as the first time she kneed him, but it still hurt.

He had been just going to check on her before he left to go to the bridge in preparation for their arrival. When she had opened her eyes and stared up at him with eyes the color of the rarest blue gems on his world, he had been lost. Her long hair had been spread about her in wild abandon, as if she had just been made love to. Her yellow dress was tangled around her long, bare legs.

He never thought about the rich color of the sands on his planet as being beautiful before, but her skin reminded him of it and he realized that the warm, tan color made his mouth water at the thought of seeing what it would be like to run his lips along her creamy, sun-kissed skin.

Those feelings brought back the anger that she appeared to have some type of influence over him. He was the one in control. Determined to prove it, he knew he was trying to intimidate her when he closed in on her, trapping her between the wall and his body. Yet, the moment he got close to her, all rational thought flew from his mind.

When she retorted with a threat of her own, his body had reacted to the challenge. He knew the moment his lips touched hers that he had made a strategic mistake. Instead of intimidating her, it had sent an explosive charge through his body that settled in his groin, hardening his balls and filling his cock until he wanted to rip his pants off and bury himself deep in her channel to satisfy the savage thirst that overwhelmed him.

His eyelids slowly lifted until he was gazing up at her flushed face. Another low groan escaped him, this time as his tender balls and cock reacted to her wide-eyed mortification. The knowledge that she hadn't kneed him on purpose helped a little.

"You… are dangerous," he informed her in a strained voice.

Her look of concern changed to a dark scowl and she pursed her lips tightly together. Amusement and desire washed through him when she curled her legs to the side and folded her arms across her chest in defiance. Even with her hair hanging about her in a messy tangle of waves and her dress creased from her journey, she still looked breathtaking.

"You really need to learn some manners," she retorted in an icy voice. "Now, may I ask why you felt it was necessary to kidnap me?"

He was about to reply when the comlink attached to his shirt pinged. Reaching up, he tapped it to silence it. Almost immediately, it pinged again. With a resigned sigh, he muttered under his breath for it to connect.

"What?" He demanded in irritation.

"We have company," Andras replied in a clipped tone. "You may want to get up to the bridge."

Ristèard cursed, sitting up with a wince. He rose to his feet in one fluid motion. His mouth tight with anger at the interruption. He glanced back down at where Ricki was still sitting, watching him intently.

"I have to go," he stated. "Stay here until I or one of my men come for you."

He watched Ricki bow her head in acknowledgement. A momentary wave of regret flashed through him that he had to involve such a delicate woman into the mess of his world, but he had sworn he would do whatever was necessary to save his planet and his people. With a sharp nod, he turned on his heel and strode from his cabin.

"Who is it?" He asked, connecting with Andras the moment the door to his cabin closed behind him.

"It would appear the council has just discovered we were missing, Councilman Manderlin is demanding permission to board," Andras replied dryly. "I could blow his transport out of the sky and say my finger slipped."

Ristèard stepped into the lift as the doors opened and turned before giving the command for it to take him to the bridge. Manderlin was new to the board.

He was older than the sands of the Eastern desert and just as persistent in getting under his skin. Why he was elected to the board, Ristèard had no idea. He expected the nosy, irritating bastard to drop dead any day.

"Don't," he impatiently ordered. "Let's find out what he wants first."

An exasperated sigh sounded over the comlink before Andras murmured his agreement. Ristèard's lips twitched at his second-in-command's impatience to blow something up. Andras' blood thirsty nature was probably one of the reasons they got along so well. They were very much alike, kill first, ask later.

The moment the lift doors opened, he swept through them. Two warriors quickly stepped out of his way and stood at attention as he passed by them. He paused for a moment, looking at them before glancing back at the lift.

"Make sure that the female in my cabin remains there," he instructed. "If anything should happen, you are responsible for keeping her safe at all cost."

Both men looked back at him with grim, determined faces. "Yes, sir," they replied, before turning and entering the open lift.

Satisfied that Ricki would be protected, he continued on his journey to the bridge. He did not have the time or the patience to deal with anyone who would destroy Elpidios for their own selfish reasons. He nodded to Andras before turning his gaze to the elderly councilman.

"Manderlin, what do you want?" Ristèard asked bluntly.

Chapter 7

Ricki leaned forward in front of the small mirror to make sure that she looked her normal, efficient self. Hair pulled back into a bun, check. Lip gloss touched up, check. Dress... Well, there was not much she could do about the wrinkles, but she had cleaned the smudges of dirt off from where she had climbed the tree. That had not been her smartest decision, but it had been the only one that she could think of when she realized how close the man had been to catching her.

"Not that it had mattered in the end," she said to her reflection. "This will just have to do. Now, to try to figure out what is going on."

Ricki started to close her purse when she saw the small crystal disk with the information she had downloaded to read. Biting her lip, she pulled it out and held it in the palm of her hand, staring at it with a frown. Glancing back into the cabin, the familiar outline of an information tablet caught her attention.

Picking up her purse, she walked back into the main area of the cabin and over to the long couch. The room was about the size of a large hotel suite back home. It contained a bed slightly larger than a super King-size bed, a small narrow table with two chairs, the couch and a matching chair positioned near what looked like a window, but upon a second glance proved to be just a screen to make it look like one and a large bathroom with a sink, toilet, and shower.

The entire thing was rather utilitarian. It was obvious it was built and designed for efficiency, not relaxation. Ricki adjusted her glasses, thankful that they hadn't been lost during her kidnapping. Crossing the room, she picked up the tablet before moving over to the table where she sat down.

Tapping it, she frown in frustration when she saw it was locked. Biting her lip, she frowned. She had the same issue back on Kassis when she was trying to access information from the archives. Indecision held her for several seconds before she opened her purse again and pulled out a second crystal disk.

She had mentioned to Stan her frustration at always having to ask for assistance from the Master Archive Librarian. The next day, Stan had given her this disk with a wink and told her to never leave home without it.

"If you want information, Ricki, this program is the magic key," Stan had teased. "Pop it in any terminal and it will open any doors you want."

Ricki didn't think it would really work, but it had. Whatever coding Stan had written, it appeared to know how to 'talk' with the coding in the archive files. She didn't know if it would work here, but it was worth a try.

Sliding the thin disk into the side of the tablet, she watched as the familiar symbols flashed across the screen. Her eyes widened in surprise and delight when she saw that she had access. She opened her purse and pulled out the slim scanner that Jazin had given her. She loved the way it worked, translating the symbols of their language into English. While it wasn't always perfect, it was close enough that she could usually comprehend what the data meant.

She glanced up at the door, suddenly feeling guilty, before shrugging. She didn't ask to be kidnapped and the tablet had been left out in the open, so it wasn't like she was doing anything wrong. Besides, she was smart enough to know when to use the resources around her to get the information she wanted.

Slipping Stan's miracle chip out, she placed it back into its protective sleeve and returned her attention to the document that was opened on the screen. It looked like some type of report. Frowning, she ran the scanner over the smooth surface, reading the words that appeared on it.

"Status: Critical," she murmured. "Generators in zones four, eight, ten, sixteen, and twenty-one are showing beginning signs of failure. Shield capacity down to forty-three percent. Additional failures expected to occur within weeks. Radiation level has increased by point zero-two percent. Recommendation: evacuation of planet. Estimated deaths...."

Ricki's voice faded at the unthinkable number of lives expected to be lost. Tears blurred her vision when she finished reading the report. It was mind boggling to think of an entire planet wiped out and the weight of despair that Ristèard Roald must be feeling.

"It must be overwhelming to be the leader of a world and know that so many depend on you," she whispered, brushing at the tear coursing down her cheek. Touching the screen, she reduced the report. Her eyes widened when she saw the screen open behind it. "What the...!"

She was staring at a mirror image of herself, yet, it wasn't. Her fingers trembled slightly as they touched the photograph of the stone carving. Moving the scanner down over the words, she hesitantly read them.

"Only known image of the Empress of Elpidios. Information transcribed from the ancient stone tablet found in the Lost City states she will return to Elpidios during its bleakest time to save it. The rest of the tablet was extensively damaged by erosion and no other information could be read," Ricki whispered, staring back up at the image of herself... the Ancient Empress. "Oh God," she moaned, shaking her head. "They think I'm their missing Empress!"

Chapter 8

Ajaska Ja Kel Coradon walked over to the small alcove in the office to pour himself a drink. He desperately needed it to curb the fire burning through him. He loved a challenge and he had definitely found one with Katarina Danshov.

He quickly downed the double shot of potent liquor he had poured. Wiping his hand across his mouth, he poured another one before turning when he heard Walter Bailey's loud, angry voice echoing in the corridor as he came closer.

"Torak, I demand you do something!" Walter bellowed in aggravation as he hurried into the room. "I demand retribution."

Ajaska glanced at his oldest son, he had passed his position as ruler of Kassis to Torak several years before. He and Torak had decided it was best for him to be involved on the Alliance Council since he already knew many of the council members from the different star systems.

Ajaska watched as Torak rose out of his chair, motioning for Walter and Nema to have a seat. Torak waited until the servant that followed Walter into the room brought in the refreshments for the Ringmaster and his tiny wife before he said anything.

"What appears to be the problem?" Torak asked.

"That huge blue bastard has kidnapped my daughter is the problem!" Walter snarled, setting his tea on the tall side table near the couch. "Stan has finally woken. He said that Ristèard Roald attacked him and Ricki last night. He fought off two men, but another one must have come up behind him and shot him full of a sedative. He wanted to know if Ricki was okay. She never returned home last night. You have to do something immediately! God only knows what that brutal bastard will do to her."

Nema reached over and tightly gripped Walter's hand. Tears glimmered in her eyes as she stared at the small group of people in the room. She looked with pleading eyes from Torak to Ajaska.

Ajaska wasn't too concerned with Ricki's disappearance. He had been briefed by his security team the moment Stan had been found. He glanced at Jazin who nodded to him and he stepped up to stand beside him.

"Were you able to confirm the information that Jarmen gave us?" Jazin asked under his breath, glancing over his shoulder at Torak before his eye's darkened when they landed on his own mate.

Jarmen D'ju was a male his youngest son, Jazin, had rescued from an illegal research facility. The man was unlike anything he had ever seen, but if Jazin trusted him, then so would he. He knew very little about him, except he was a ghost who moved in the shadows. Jazin mentioned the two had been working on a number of different defense systems and that Jarmen would be leaving soon.

"Yes, I spoke briefly with Ristèard," Ajaska whispered, watching with amusement as Torak became distracted when River entered the room. He had always hoped that his sons would find their mate. There was no denying Torak had found his in River. For a moment, the image of a dark haired, fire-breathing hellcat flashed through his mind. His fingers moved absently to the long, narrow slits in his shirt even as a grin curved his lips. "He admitted that he kidnapped Ricki."

Jazin frowned at his father's amusement. "Well, did you tell him he needed to bring her back? You know that we offered protection to all the humans. Manota warned him when he was here that Ricki was under the protection of the royal family."

"Ristèard may be a cold, brutal bastard, but he is also a fair one," Ajaska murmured. "He won't hurt her."

"So, you are just going to let him take her?" Jazin asked in disbelief.

"Of course not," Ajaska replied with a grin, listening as Walter demanded Torak to do something about his daughter's kidnapping.

"What about my daughter?" Walter demanded, standing up and waving his short arms in the air in aggravation. "What are you going to do?"

Ajaska shook his head and grinned at Jazin. "Kidnap her back," he replied loud enough for everyone in the room to hear. "Right from under his royal blue nose."

* * *

Ristèard stared at the elderly councilman in frustration. Manderlin had come to warn him that another plot was underway to kill him. He turned to stare out the viewport, his mind churning with fury. It had been dangerous for him to leave Elpidios at this volatile time, but his hands had been tied.

He was scheduled to meet with the rest of the council in less than two hours. Manderlin had come to warn him that several of the councilmen were pushing to have him and his elite security guard arrested for treason. Treason!

"Who is pushing it?" Ristèard demanded, not turning around.

A tired sigh escaped Manderlin. "Texla and Raomlin," the elderly councilman replied. "But, I do not think they are the ones who started it. There is someone else influencing them. You said that the Kassisan traitor was killed almost a month ago, did you not? I fear he is not the only one."

Ristèard turned at Manderlin's softly spoken words. He could tell the man didn't realize that he had spoken aloud. His eyes narrowed on the wrinkled face, noting the lines of fatigue and stress.

"What are you not telling me?" He demanded in a cold voice. "Why do you think the council is working with someone else?"

Ristèard took a step toward where Manderlin had sunk down in the chair at the table in the command room. He was determined to get to the bottom of the constant threats that had increased over the past six months. Turning, he looked over his shoulder with an irritated scowl when the door to the room suddenly opened. Harald stood in the entrance, staring at him with a resigned expression.

"What is it now?" Ristèard demanded in frustration.

He saw Harald grimace at the sharp tone in his voice. It took a moment to realize why Harald had interrupted him after he had instructed him not to let anyone in. There was a shimmer of sunlight colored hair barely visible over Harald's right shoulder, testament to why his trusted guard had ignored his order.

"She demanded to see you," Harald replied, stepping to the side with an apologetic glance.

Ristèard turned his scowl on Ricki. The dark look deepened when all she did was raise one delicate eyebrow at him and stepped past Harald with a polite murmur of thanks. What the hell was she doing out of his cabin? He would have the heads of the two men he had assigned to keep her there.

"What are you doing here?" He snapped. Almost immediately, he regretted his harsh tone. He shifted uneasily when she continued into the room, looking him in the eye while pressing her lips tightly together in disapproval at his tone. "It isn't safe for you to be roaming the ship," he muttered when she stopped a short distance from him.

His eyes swept over her, taking in every minute detail. Her hair was back into the familiar, upward twist that she always wore. His fingers actually twitched and he had to clench them into a fist to keep from reaching out and pulling it loose again. She had smoothed out the wrinkles in her dress and had her matching carry bag on one shoulder. His gaze swept over her willowy figure, pausing on the tablet in her hands. It looked suspiciously like his. His gaze returned to her face and he almost winced when she released a heavy sigh. How the release of a breath could say so much, he would never understand, but he could almost feel her exasperation with him in it.

"How do you do?" Ricki asked, turning away from him to focus on Manderlin. "I'm Ricki Bailey. I hope I'm not interrupting anything too important, but it was imperative that I speak with Grand Ruler Roald. I hope you'll forgive my intrusion."

Ristèard folded his arms across his chest as he watched Ricki. She was shaking the bemused councilman's hand and chatting with him, asking him what his position was and where he was from. She even asked him about his family! Irritation and frustration flashed through him when he saw the crusty old bastard smile at her in return. He was about to say something when she turned to look at him.

"I truly am sorry to have interrupted your meeting, but what I have to say couldn't wait. I read the report that was sent to you and several things reminded me of some recent information I had read about back on Kassis," Ricki explained, looking him in the eye with a very serious expression. "While I don't have a clear picture yet, I believe it might be relevant to the situation at hand."

"Situation?" Ristèard asked, frowning. He glanced uneasily at Manderlin. "Which report are you talking about and how did you get access to my login?"

He watched Ricki calmly reach up and adjust her glasses. A silent curse flashed through his mind when his fingers twitched again. What was it about this female that made him want to mess up her cool, touch-me-not, composure?

"You're looking like a little boy denied a chance to put a frog down the front of a girl's top," she murmured, pressing her lips together when his eyes immediately zoomed in on the front of her dress. "I would not recommend it."

"Recommend what?" Ristèard asked in a husky voice.

He reluctantly dragged his eyes away from the modest cut of her dress and back to her face. A slight, unfamiliar flush stained his cheeks when he saw the amusement fighting with a tint of worry.

She shook her head. "I came because I read a section in the report that triggered a memory of something else I had come across when researching the history of Kassis," she explained. "Is this information I should share with you in private, or can the other gentlemen also be included? Personally, I think it might be better if Councilman Manderlin were to remain as it pertains to an area he might be more familiar with than you."

Ristèard glanced over his shoulder where Andras was leaning back against the wall, silently watching everything that was happening, before he turned his attention back to Manderlin. The elderly councilman was staring at Ricki with an awed expression on his face. Curiosity fought with his natural instinct for privacy. A surprising sense of admiration filled him when he saw that she was patiently waiting for his answer. In the short period of time since he had first met her, he was discovering more and more about her personality and character that he not only admired, but trusted, something reserved for only a few select people close to him. She did not try to convince him, but instead waited for his decision.

He nodded, surprising himself. "Go ahead," he replied with a jerk of his head.

"Thank you," she said with a slight bow of her head. "Perhaps a short background will help you understand my methodology and why I believe there is a connection to the archived data from Kassis and the current situation on Elpidios. Back home on my world, one of my specialties was being able to read through, interpret, and organize large amounts of information so that I could determine the most efficient way to handle any issues before they could occur. I found having advanced knowledge of the countries we were traveling to tremendously helped me when dealing with the local governments. It often helped to prevent any unnecessary problems that could arise when dealing with the different cultures. It also gave me a better understanding of their laws and how to make sure that we did not violate any of them."

Ristèard reached over and pulled out the chair next to Ricki, motioning for her to sit down and continue with her explanation. Once she was seated, he moved around the table and took the chair opposite her so he could study her face as she talked. He discretely touched a button on the controller attached to the belt around his waist. His eyes flickered to the tablet Ricki was holding. Some instinct told him to record what she was about to share for future reference. One thing he had learned long ago was to never take his gut feelings for granted. It had saved his life, and the lives of his men, on too many occasions.

"Continue," Ristèard said, folding his arms across his chest and sitting back in his seat.

Chapter 9

Ricki drew in a deep, steadying breath before she glanced across the table at Ristèard. It had taken her almost an hour to skim through the information she had already read and piece the timelines together to see if it made any sense. Granted, she needed to do more research, primarily on the Elpidios side, but she felt confident that what she had read was related.

Breaking contact with Ristèard's intense stare, she gazed down at the tablet in her hands. Setting it on the table in front of her, she glanced around the room trying to decide the best way to convey what she had learned so far. A short history lesson of Kassis was necessary to understand the interconnection to Elpidios.

"I'm not sure how much you know about Kassisan history so I'll give you a short overview. Over a thousand years ago, there was an intense battle between the primitive people on Kassis and an alien race. The race was never identified, but from the documented sketches and descriptions, it would appear that it was a type of Mantodea family, almost like an overgrown Praying Mantas back on Earth. There was a description of a second species involved, but I need more time to understand how that could be. From the records I've reviewed, this caught my attention *'The red dissolved until the ground glowed with the lighted crystals. All around her were the glittering stones. New life grew around her as the crystals absorbed into the ground, growing and spreading'.* I think there is a correlation between the blood of the species and the crystals on Kassis."

"That is all well and good, but how is that supposed to help us?" Andras asked, straightening from where he was leaning against the wall. "Those species haven't been seen in over a thousand years."

"True," Ricki responded, looking down at the tablet again with a frown. "But it is a clue as to where the crystals came from. What I found curious was that the crystals absorbed into the ground, growing and spreading. If that is the case, what happened to all the crystals on your world?"

Ristèard leaned forward and clasped his hands together. His face was tight with regret. He looked at Andras when he stepped forward.

"Other species valued the power held within the crystals. Unlike the Kassis crystals which grow quickly, ours did not. It wasn't until several centuries ago that it was discovered how valuable the crystals were to the survival of our planet. Once the reason for the increase in radiation was understood, my grandfather put a ban on exporting it off the planet. Unfortunately, there were others who gained great wealth from selling it," Ristéard explained.

Ricki nodded in understanding. "We have the same issues back on Earth," she quietly replied. "Extensive development of certain lands and the stripping of natural resources has caused problems. Fortunately, there are people who are working to reverse some of the damage done."

"Yes, but your planet is now...," Manderlin started to say, pausing when Ristéard shook his head. "Yes, well, I'm afraid if something isn't done soon, millions will perish." He turned and looked at Ricki with an assessing gaze before returning his attention to Ristéard. "I know there are those on the council that oppose you and wish to overthrow you, Grand Ruler, but I have no such desire. I fought beside your grandfather when we were boys. He was a proud man and I respected him. The only reason I was voted onto the council was because the others thought I was too old to be a threat. I may be old," he added with a twinkle in his eyes, "but, I am far from being dead."

Ricki's light, amused laughter filled the air, pulling an immediate response from him. She grinned at the elderly councilman, looking at him with a warmth that made Ristéard wish she were gazing at him instead.

"The reason I suggested that Councilman Manderlin remain is because I think there might be more hidden in the ancient city," Ricki admitted in a soft voice, turning to stare at Ristéard. "I was reading over the report you had from the scientists studying the ancient city where the tablet was found. There was a set of symbols on the side of the tablet."

Ristéard waved his hand in dismissal. "I know. Rue and his mate stated it was too damaged to interpret," he interrupted.

"It is true that most of the symbol was eroded, but not all of it," Ricki stated. "There was enough of it to recognize the symbols. I was able to match them to the tablet found by the Kassisan scientists."

Ristéard frowned, studying Ricki's determined face. "What do you mean 'enough to recognize'?" He asked, staring at her intently.

Ricki's eyes locked with his for what seemed like minutes, when in fact it was mere seconds. He saw the intelligence, the determination, and the trace of stubbornness that re-enforced his belief that he had made the right decision to kidnap her. The strange feelings that had plagued him ever since he saw her standing in the large tent back on Kassis swept through him. What was it about her that kept him off-balance?

He watched as she forced her eyes to break contact. She slid the tablet in front of her across the table. He glanced down at it. His gaze locked on the side-by-side images. One was a more intact tablet. He couldn't read the ancient writing, but the writing was very similar. Running vertically along the side was another set of symbols. He glanced at the ones on the intact tablet before glancing at the tablet found in the Eastern desert. The first ten symbols were identical.

"What do they mean?" He murmured in fascination.

"I think they are coordinates," Ricki replied. "I've used the key the scientist used to decipher the tablet. If you touch the bottom, it will show you what I believe the damaged message says. It is a series of numbers. I took the liberty of plugging the numbers into the map you have on your tablet and it pinpointed a location not far from the underground city that was marked on the map."

Ristéard scowled at Ricki. "You know that was secured information you were reading, don't you? I am the only one who had access to it," he stated, sitting back and folding his arms. "Remind me to ask you when we are alone how you were able to not only log in to my tablet, but how you were able to access classified data as well."

His fingers curled around the tablet in his hands when she gave him a serene, non-committal smile. Frowning, he gazed down at the tablet again. She was right. The coordinates pointed to a mountain ridge just twenty kilometers from the entrance to the ancient city. It looked as if his unwilling Empress was living up to the legend surrounding her.

*** * ***

A half hour later, Ristèard seemed convinced by her findings. She had continued to elaborate on the similarity between the tablet found by the Kassisans and the one found on Elpidios and the conclusion that she had drawn from information she had been able to piece together so far. She really would need more time to research the Elpidios' archives. There had to be additional files that contained more about the history of the aliens that had come to the planet and why the two tablets contained the same coordinates.

Her mind switched gears to the man who had kidnapped her as they stepped out of the conference room and onto the main part of the bridge. She refused to be intimidated by him. He had a very strong, commanding personality. After reading the report and piecing together facts that she already knew about him, she could understand why that was necessary. Still, some instinct told her that it was important that she not let him walk all over her, not that she would in the first place. Her own personality was one of control. While she wasn't as aggressive and in-your-face as he was, she was still very tenacious when she set her mind to something. She would think of him as just another task that needed to be completed. While the looks he kept giving her were disturbing, they were nothing she couldn't handle. Adjusting her glasses, she nodded to the other male who had remained a primarily silent observer as she passed him in the doorway leading out onto the bridge.

She couldn't resist looking around the large room. For a moment, her gaze paused on the two men that had escorted her to Ristéard. She gave them both a reassuring smile when she noticed the nervous glances they kept casting at the large man standing next to her.

Both had insisted that she remain in his cabin, but she had persisted, telling them both that it was a matter of life or death. Ricki knew she could be rather intimidating herself when she wanted something. Her mom and dad referred to it as 'the look'. It might not be the greatest talent in the circus, but it had helped them hundreds of times.

A giggle escaped her when she thought of a few of those times. Her eyes danced with mischief when she caught Ristéard's questioning glance. Shrugging her shoulders, she continued her assessment of the Warship.

"I've never been on the bridge of a spaceship before," she remarked, looking around her. "When we were on Manota's ship, we were restricted primarily to the lower sections, except when we were attacked. That was pretty scary."

"You were attacked?" Ristéard asked in surprise. "By who? It is very unusual for anyone to attack a Warship, even one traveling alone. The Kassisan warships are known for their advanced weaponry."

"Yes, well, that didn't stop you from coming to Kassis and kidnapping me, now did it?" Ricki retorted. "The technology is mind-boggling. The Earth isn't nearly as advanced."

"Yes, that is what I have heard," Ristéard replied in an uneasy voice. "I must admit, from what I have recently learned, I am surprised that you and the others of your kind were so receptive to the idea of aliens."

Ricki studied the half dozen men and women working quietly at their assigned stations. There were two sitting at a console in the front. Behind them, Andras, the man from the conference room, had moved to sit in what looked like the captain's chair. The other man, Harald, nodded to them both as he passed by and exited the bridge. There were others at different stations, monitoring screens and talking quietly.

Ricki chuckled as she nodded. "There were several things that helped, I think," she absently responded. "One, Jo had returned with Manota. She trusted him and he brought her home. How can anyone be bad if they do that? The second thing I think that made the biggest difference is that most of the members of the circus are rather strange and unusual themselves. It wasn't that difficult to accept an alien any more than it was to accept Katarina, Mattie, Marcus, Stan, my parents, or the countless others. I mean, look at Marvin and Martin! They have been with the circus for almost ten years and we never suspected they were aliens."

"The Kor d'lurs are known for being able to blend in. That is how they study other species," he commented with a shrug. "The information they bring back is very useful, such as…"

Ricki raised her eyebrow at him in question when his voice faded and all he did was shrug again. It was as if he suddenly decided that he had said too much. If he was worried that she or any of the others in the circus would hold the fact that Marvin and Martin were alien against them, he needn't have worried. They had proven they were fair and decent individuals, especially to her. They had been incredibly protective of her parents and her over the years. Everyone loved them.

Well, except for Thea right now, she thought with a sigh. *Thea was still deeply hurt by their lack of trust.*

Ricki started when she felt the warmth of Ristèard's hand through the thin cloth of her dress as he wrapped his arm around her and drew her so close she was pressed against his side. A low squeak escaped her when his hand slid up under the yellow sweater she was wearing and ran his thumb along her skin where the dress dipped in the back. The heat from his touch seared through the rest of the material as if she wasn't wearing anything at all. She silently cursed when she felt a matching heat blossom inside her and spread from the core of her womanhood all the way up to her cheeks.

"You are feeling... well?" He asked in a husky tone, leaning closer so he could whisper in her ear as he guided her off the bridge. "Perhaps you should rest. We will be arriving on Elpidios soon."

Ricki wrapped the fingers of her right hand around the strap of her purse while using her left hand to straighten her glasses. She would be damned if she let him know that his touch was affecting her in any way. Stiffening her shoulders, she pulled away from him, taking an additional two steps to the side for good measure.

"I feel perfectly well, thank you," she replied in a frosty tone. "I'm just not accustomed to someone constantly being in my personal space. I don't remember reading anything about this being a habit of your culture."

She knew immediately that it wasn't customary the minute she saw the wicked grin that curved his lips. "It's not," he informed her, reaching out and wrapping his hand around her right arm so he could turn her around. "But, you should get used to it," he added, backing her up until she was pressed against the wall just outside the bridge.

Panic swept through her before it was replaced with icy determination when she saw several warriors' grin at her when they passed by. Even standing as straight and rigid as she could, she still had to look up into his dark silver eyes. Mischief and heated desire blazed from them.

"I wouldn't if I were you," she warned with an icy tone. "I demand that you step back."

"And if I don't," he replied in a low, thick voice filled with promise. "What will you do?"

Chapter 10

Ristèard glared over at Ricki, wincing as the healer touched the knot on the back of his head with the scanner. He absently rubbed the center of his chest and the scowl on his face turned even darker. She briefly glanced at him before returning her attention to the tablet he had dropped when she had knocked him on his ass… again.

"I want you to know I have killed for less than what you did." Wincing again, he glared at the healer. "Be careful!"

He turned to scowl at Ricki. The scowl faded to one of wariness when she released a long, exasperated sigh and set the tablet down on the table next to her before she stood up. He straightened from where he had been leaning forward so the healer could look at the bump on his head.

"Go," he ordered.

"Grand Ruler," the healer started to say before he pulled away with a curt nod when Ristèard shot him a look of warning. "If you feel any dizziness, call me."

"Thank you, Karis," Ricki said politely. "I'm sure his head is too hard to have been hurt that bad."

Ristèard grunted and mumbled under his breath that his head *wasn't* that hard. His eyes glared at Ricki when she covered the chuckle that escaped her behind a fake cough. His head hurt and so did his chest where she had pressed that damn cylinder to it.

Ricki pursed her lips together and placed her hands on her hips. He shifted on the chair where Sadao and Emyr had placed him after they scraped him up off the floor.

"Do you have any other weapons on you?" He demanded, his gaze flickering warily to her hands before returning them to her face.

"If I did, I wouldn't admit it," Ricki retorted with a roll of her eyes, thinking of the small device Marcus had given her. It had been basically a single shot paintball gun, powerful enough that when it was discharged at close range to knock someone on their ass and give them a bruise. The fact that had hit his head hard on a service droid that was in the corridor behind him had been unexpected. She had just been trying to put some space between them and let him know that she wasn't totally defenseless. "I warned you to keep out of my personal space."

Ristèard's mouth tightened into a stubborn line. "And I told you that I was claiming you," he stated, standing up and folding his arms arrogantly across his chest. "We will be on Elpidios within the hour. I will have Sadao escort you to my cabin until it is time for us to transport down. This time, I suggest you stay there."

He watched in satisfaction as her mouth dropped open before she snapped it shut. "I need to contact my father and mother and let them know where I am and that I am alright," she seethed. "And for your information, I have decided to do what I can to help you, but that does not mean I agree to any of this foolishness. I'm not even certain I can help you more than the small amount of information I've been able to remember and piece together. I'm sure your scientists or scholars can do a much better job than I can. I think it might be better, after all, to return me to Kassis or at least notify Torak, Jazin, or Manota so one of them can come get me."

Ristèard ignored Ricki's last statement. No one was going to be taking her anywhere. Ricki had ignited a fire in his blood that he needed to calm before he returned her to Kassis. While he might have a hard time believing she was truly his 'prophesied' Empress, that didn't mean he wasn't curious about her. He was determined to figure out why every time he was around her, his carefully controlled emotions turned into mass chaos.

At the moment, he had too much to do, not to mention a throbbing headache to get rid of, to contend with Ricki's actions or her demands. He would deal with her after he settled the newest turmoil among the council. Calling for Sadao, he waited until the other man entered the room before speaking.

"Take her to my cabin and keep her there," Ristèard ordered, never taking his eyes off of Ricki's face. "Do not let her out until I tell you. I am holding you responsible for her safety."

Sadao glanced uneasily back and forth. There was no way to miss the tension that filled the medical unit. He nodded, moving to the side of the door when Ristèard took a step forward.

"I need to contact my parents," Ricki pleaded in a low voice, tilting her head to one side so she could look up at him. She lightly touched his arm when he paused next to her. "Please. I don't want them to worry."

Ristèard's eyes narrowed as he looked into her pale, blue eyes. A wave of determination, and a touch of desperation, swept through him. He ignored Sadao's raised eyebrow.

"For a kiss," he said. "Kiss me and I will inform your parents that you are safe."

"Kiss...," Ricki whispered in shock, blinking several times and shaking her head as if she couldn't quite believe what she had just heard. "Why, that's... That's... Blackmail!"

"Take it or leave it. Your parents will never know for sure what happened to you otherwise," Ristèard replied with a shrug of his broad shoulders. "Personally, I could care less."

Ricki's swiftly inhaled breath echoed loudly through the room. A dark flush stained her cheeks. Ristèard suspected it was caused more from anger than from passion. Still, he was desperate enough to take even that emotion. After all, he reasoned, anger and passion were two halves of a whole if fanned correctly.

"You are a despicable bastard," Ricki hissed out under her breath. "A horrible, arrogant..."

Ristèard's eyes glittered with a fierce warning as he turned and gripped her forearms. He pulled her closer, but did not bend down to capture her lips even though everything inside him begged for him to do so. He wanted her to be the one to reach out to him. He didn't care if he had to use blackmail to get her to do it. He just wanted, needed, her to kiss him for once.

"It is your choice," he replied, suddenly releasing her and stepping back with a nod. "Take her."

Satisfaction burst through him when she held her hand out to Sadao. "Alright, but…." She paused and looked at Sadao before turning back to him. "But, I would prefer not to have an audience if you don't mind," she stated in a husky voice.

"Wait outside the door," Ristèard ordered, not looking at Sadao.

Neither one of them moved until the door closed behind Sadao. Only when they were alone did Ricki step closer to him. For a fraction of a second, Ristèard felt a wave of unease wash through him. Perhaps he should have thought through his demand before making it. Pushing the errant thought away, he waited.

"You know I'm doing this out of duress, don't you?" She murmured in a soft, husky voice as she placed her hands on his shoulders and rose up on her toes. "…Complete and utter duress."

Ristèard swallowed and started to reply before a burst of exploding emotions swamped all rational thought as Ricki pressed her lips to his, in a sensual kiss that made his toes curl. His lips automatically parted when she touched her tongue to them. After that, chaos reigned as it hit him with a force that shattered the protective wall he had built around his heart.

For the love of the Goddess, he thought in stunned disbelief when she wrapped her arms around his neck and deepened the kiss. *I don't think I will ever get enough of this.*

..*

Ricki couldn't believe it when Ristèard demanded she kiss him in exchange for contacting her parents and letting them know she was safe. Her first thought had been to inform him where he could shove his demand. Again, her instinct for handling situations told her that she would best accomplish what she needed to do with a more diplomatic approach.

If he wants a kiss, she decided. *I'll give him a kiss that will knock his socks off.*

While she might not have had extensive lessons on kissing, she figured it couldn't be all that difficult. She would just imagine he was someone whom she would really want to kiss. Someone tall. Someone who made her feel feminine and fragile.

Someone, okay, someone like him, but not like him, she decided as she stepped closer.

Licking her lips to moisten them, she slid her hands up to his shoulders. A fierce wave of determination and empowerment flooded her when she saw the look of unease and doubt flash across his face at her softly murmured words. Good, it would serve him right to feel uneasy.

"You know I'm doing this out of duress, don't you?" She murmured, not meaning a single word of it as she rose up on her toes. "… Complete and utter duress."

She captured his lips in a heated kiss, pouring every ounce of her rage into it. *Okay,* she thought vaguely, touching her tongue to his firm, smooth lips in an effort to deepen the kiss, *maybe rage was a little too intense a word.*

Still, she wanted to teach him a lesson he wouldn't forget, namely, don't mess with Ricki Bailey! She wasn't some pansy who crumbled at a challenge. She had taken the circus all the way around the world, to just about every inhabited continent, and just about every country on Earth.

There wasn't a diplomat alive who could outsmart her when it came to finding a loophole or two. If he thought demanding a kiss would intimidate her, then it was time to show him who he was up against. She was a Master Chess player, and thanks to Marvin and Martin, an even better Poker player. She knew when to bluff and could carry it off against the best players in the world.

Threading her fingers through his short hair, she tilted her head and opened her mouth wider so she could tease his tongue with hers. She ran the tip of her tongue along the edge of his teeth. A low, guttural moan escaped him at the same time as a shudder ran through his body and his arms wrapped tightly around her waist.

Ricki let her body melt against his. She decided if she was going to show him that she could give as good as he gave, she might as well totally go for the gold. By the time she was done with him, he'd be eating out of the palm of her hand. She just hoped that it didn't end up being the other way around.

Raising her right leg up, she rubbed the inside of her thigh against his and dragged her nails along his scalp in a gentle massage. Another shudder ran through him, giving her the courage to continue.

Small explosions of pleasure burst through Ricki, making her crave more when he responded to her gentle exploration. Her body instinctively pressed closer to his, seeking his warmth. A small gasp escaped her when the position of moving her leg up caused his aroused cock to press against her. Rational thought returned, making her realize just how dangerous a game she was playing. Especially when she felt his hands moving along her back and her ass.

The kiss had turned out to be far different than she expected. She had never felt such a charge of emotion or need before. She slowly ended it with a sigh of regret. Unable to resist, she nipped his bottom lip between her teeth before she drew in a deep breath.

Ricki slid her leg down along his until she was standing on her own two feet again instead of being plastered against him. Glancing up at his tense face, she couldn't resist pressing another kiss to the corner of his mouth before she pulled away from him and took several unsteady steps back.

She stared up at his flushed face. It was a darker blue and there was a pulse throbbing in his cheek, as if he was barely holding onto his control. Her gaze swept down to his hands, which were clenched into tight fists at his side.

It took a moment for her to realize that his hands had been busy as well. Her hair swung freely down her back. She had no idea what had happened to her hair pins. Luckily, she always carried extra in her purse.

Swallowing, she opened her purse and pulled out a pencil instead. Her hands were shaking too much to bother with hair pins. Snapping her purse shut, she grabbed her long hair and twisted it up.

"Don't," he ordered in a guttural voice filled with desire.

Ricki raised her eyebrow at him and finished the twist. Once it was in a bun, she stabbed the pencil through her hair to temporarily hold it in place until she could do something a little more refined. The main thing right now was to make sure he didn't realize how much the kiss had affected her. She would have a meltdown once she was alone.

Satisfied that her hair was once again contained, she lifted her chin and stared back at him with a cool, calm expression. He would never guess that she didn't have a Royal Flush. Pasting a serene smile on her lips, she ignored the fact that his face was turning an even darker blue than before.

"I expect you to keep your promise about notifying my parents and assuring them that I am well," Ricki stated, wrapping her fingers around the strap of her purse. "I would also appreciate a timeline as to my return. Now, if you will excuse me, I do believe I will freshen up before our departure."

She breathed out a sigh of relief when the door behind her suddenly opened and Andras and Sadao stood in the opening. Turning on her heel, she walked out of the door. She didn't bother to see if Sadao followed her or not. She remembered the way back to Ristèard's cabin. Right now, she needed to put distance between her and Ristèard.

It was only when she was several yards down the corridor that she remembered that she had forgotten to grab the tablet off the table where she had set it. Slowing, she turned slightly and waited for Sadao. Drawing in a steadying breath, she smiled politely at him.

"Your name is Sadao, isn't it?" She asked politely.

Sadao nodded, looking at her with a wary expression. Andras had already warned him to watch out for this female, that she wasn't all she appeared to be. He had a strange feeling about her as well. There was something different. He couldn't put his finger on it, but there was definitely something unusual about her.

"Yes," he replied.

Biting her bottom lip, Ricki looked back toward the medical unit. She didn't want to go back inside where Ristèard and Andras were, but she wanted to do more research. Making a decision, she looked back at Sadao.

"I need a tablet," she stated, raising her hand when he started to say something. "Please. I understand your hesitation, but from what I've read, your world is on the verge of a major disaster. I've been able to find some useful information, but I need to do more research. I'm very good at it. I know there is something I am missing, I can feel it. Please," she pleaded. "I know I can help."

She grinned when Sadao released a low curse and gave her a sharp nod. "You better not try anything to harm Ristèard or my people or I swear I'll cut you down myself," he growled in a low voice.

Ricki's smile faded, but she didn't look away. Instead, she stepped closer and laid her hand on his arm and waited until he looked into her eyes. There was too much riding on her finding some additional information.

"I am very good at what I do," she promised. "If there is any information that might help save your world, I can find it. I know I can."

Sadao reached up and gripped her forearm. "Come with me," he said, looking over his shoulder. "The main computers are faster and easier to use."

Ricki nodded, turning as he continued to hold her arm and hurried beside him. She refused to think about what would happen if she failed. She had read the reports, seen the numbers, and knew that for once, she was the one who must perform like she had never performed before.

A moment of anguish filled her at the thought of what Ristèard must feel at having such a heavy burden on his shoulders. She had seen how much her father had fretted during some of the leaner times when the circus was still small and struggling to stay alive.

Her dad felt responsible for every member of the cast and crew. She couldn't fathom what it would be like to have millions of lives and the existence of a planet on her shoulders. It was a weight no one should bear alone.

Chapter 11

Ristèard grimaced at Andras before turning back toward the chair he had been sitting in. He sat down and leaned forward, resting his elbows on his knees. Closing his eyes, he waited as Karis, who had stepped back into the room as well, picked up the scanner and finished working on healing the slight knot on the back of his head.

A light grunt escaped him as the headache that had been building dissolved as well. He opened his eyes and nodded to Karis. Sitting back in the chair, he waited for the healer to leave again before he directed his attention to Andras.

"What did you find out?" He asked.

Andras' lips twitched. "About what? The female or Texla and Raomlin?" He asked in return.

Ristèard scowled and stood up, rotating his shoulders. He knew what Andras was referring to. His second-in-command wanted to know how a female as delicate and obviously untrained as Ricki, could put him on his ass. He knew the answer. He couldn't seem to think straight when he was around her and had underestimated her once again.

"Texla and Raomlin," he growled.

The grin on Andras' lips faded. "They are weak. If I had to guess, they are someone's puppets," he replied. "The problem is finding out whose. They always keep a large group of warriors around them.

There has been an increase in activity within their respective zones."

Ristèard's eyes narrowed. "What type of activity? Weapons?"

Andras just nodded. "My sources say they will make a move to discredit you today at the meeting and seek control over the military," he added.

Ristèard didn't reply. It was nothing he hadn't already suspected. There had been one attempt after another over the past several years to take control of the government and eliminate him and those closest to him. It had started to increase six months ago after the discovery and release of the tablet which contain the image of the Empress of Elpidios along with the prophecy stating that the Empress would bring salvation to their world. Now that he was forging an alliance with the Kassisan Royal House, it would appear those wishing to overthrow him were getting desperate.

"Make preparations for departure," he ordered, glancing at Andras. "And, Andras…"

"Yes."

"Whatever happens, your first priority is now to protect Ricki Bailey," Ristèard said with an intense stare. "Something tells me she will be in extreme danger."

"You know I've sworn to protect you, Ristèard. Elpidios needs you," Andras interjected with a frown.

Ristèard shook his head. "My gut is telling me that it needs Ricki," he reluctantly admitted. "Once the council sees her, they will know that the prophecy is coming true. Everyone has seen the image on the tablet that the Rues discovered'. She brings hope to a dying world. If nothing else, that will cause a reaction."

"Do you think it is true?" Andras asked in a quiet voice. "Do you really think she is the Empress of Elpidios?"

Ristèard thought for several moments. His mind flashed back to the kiss he had demanded just a few minutes earlier. The intensity of it had shaken him, something that had never happened before. His first thought had been that the emotions were just lust, but he knew he was lying to himself. The pleasure, and his reaction to her touch, had been too intense.

She had shaken him to his core. He had a dozen women willing and ready should he need relief, yet he hadn't been able to stand the touch of any of them since he met Ricki. He couldn't help comparing them to her unusual beauty and he felt a wave of distaste at the idea of even touching them. Even his consort, Cherissa, couldn't entice him and had been shocked when he had immediately dismissed her.

"Ristèard," Andras repeated. "Do you really think she is the Empress?"

Ristèard jerked back to the present, turning to look back at Andras. "Yes," he said with an intense expression. "Yes, I not only think she is the prophesied Empress of Elpidios. I think she might just save our world."

Andras surprised hiss echoed in the room. "Then, I will inform the others that she is to be protected above all else," he finally agreed. "Even yourself."

* * *

Ristèard paused outside the door to his cabin. Sadao straightened from where he had been leaning back against the wall. He knew that Sadao had something on his mind. When that happened, he generally heard about it.

"She isn't what she appears," Sadao stated with a grim, determined look on his face. "There is something about her I can't put my finger on."

"She's human," Ristèard replied. "How many humans have you ever met?"

Sadao grunted and sighed. "True," he admitted. "Until we arrived on Kassis, none. I just can't help but feel there is something else about her."

"She is the Empress of Elpidios," Ristèard murmured in a low voice. "I've instructed Andras that she is to be protected at all cost."

Sadao nodded. "I figured as much when I saw her," he said. "Out of the five of us, I've always been the more superstitious. Even so, this has taken me by surprise and…"

Ristèard's eyebrow rose when Sadao's voice faded and he glanced uneasily at the door. "And…?" He asked.

Sadao gazed back at him before looking down at the floor. Ristèard could see the confusion on his friend's face and understood. He was feeling it as well. How was it possible that a two thousand year old tablet could predict the future?

Sadao finally looked back up at him before replying. "And given me hope for our world," he finished in a quiet voice. "I think she might find the answer we need."

"I do, too," Ristèard finally admitted. "I do, too."

A slow smile creased Sadao's face. "I'll protect her," he promised. "For the first time in my life, I believe there is a chance for a future."

Ristèard's throat tightened with emotion. He had never thought about a future. His life had been one about survival. He had devoted his life to finding a way to save his world. In the process, it had meant staying alive long enough to see that happened.

Now… Now even he felt a small ray of hope beginning to blossom deep inside him. He murmured for Sadao check in with Andras and to coordinate with Emyr and Harald on providing continuous coverage for Ricki when he wasn't with her. He watched as Sadao took off down the corridor before he turned back to the door of his cabin and gave the command for it to open.

What would it be like to have a future? He wondered before his gaze was captured by the unusual figure sitting on the couch in his cabin. *A future with Ricki.*

In that instant, he could see it. He could see a future with Ricki. He could see… Shaking his head, he blinked several times when he suddenly realized that she had said something.

"What?" He asked, a scowl darkening his face at being caught off guard yet again. "How do you do that?"

Ricki frowned at him, setting the tablet in her hands down on the cushion of the couch and stood up. "I asked if you are alright? You had this funny look on your face. And, how do I do what?" She asked in confusion.

Ristèard ran his hand through his hair, grateful that his head didn't hurt anymore. His lips tightened with resolve. He needed to instruct Ricki on a few things before they left the warship. The crew aboard it had been carefully picked by him and his men. Once they left it, he could not guarantee who could be trusted.

"Whenever I'm around you I can't think straight," he confessed. "This has never happened before. What strange powers do you humans have?"

He saw Ricki's eyes soften with amusement. "I'm afraid the only powers I have are the ability to be very organized and finding out information. Nothing spectacular, I assure you," she chuckled. "Although, I must admit that no one has ever told me before that they couldn't think straight around me. I might have to add that to my resume."

Desire flared inside him again at her teasing admission. He walked toward her, wondering vaguely if he kissed her again if it would be as intense as the last time. Images of the two of them entwined, his dark skin against her fair solidified in his mind.

Frustration at not having the time to make the images a reality burned through him.

Tonight, he thought.

He would claim Ricki as his Empress before the council and the world. It would give him the edge he needed to separate the traitorous members of the council once and for all. There was no doubt in his mind that whoever had been orchestrating the attacks against him would strike out in an effort to stop him.

He would also take care of the persistent, aggravating ache inside him that had been building since he first saw her. It was ridiculous for him to be behaving so irrationally. Surely once he had sated the hunger burning inside him, he would feel more in control.

Of course, then his life would be sealed to Ricki's forever, but he would deal with that later. Right now, he just wanted to kill the traitors, save his planet, and bury himself as far as he could go inside Ricki Bailey, and not necessarily in that order.

It doesn't hurt that the more I am around her, the more I want her either, he thought pausing in front of her. *Once I've bedded her, that should take care of all these strange feelings. The first thing I will do is take all of the clips she uses to hold her hair up. I don't ever want it pinned back again.*

The amusement in her eyes turned to wariness as she looked up at him. He refused to release her gaze as he bent down to capture her lips. Surprise gripped him when he found a delicate hand pressed against his mouth.

"One kiss," Ricki said sternly. "That was all you asked for in return for contacting my parents. There was never a negotiation for a second one."

Ristèard growled against her palm. A flush rose up over his cheeks when she continued to stare at him with a raised eyebrow. Out of spite, he reached up and pulled the pencil out of her hair, causing her hair to fall in silky waves down her back.

Satisfaction coursed through him when she emitted an exasperated sigh and pulled her hand away to grab the pencil he was holding out to the side. She emitted a low growl of her own when she realized that his arm was longer than hers. Taking advantage of her distraction, he wrapped his other arm around her waist and pulled her against his body. He wanted her to feel the reaction he had to her.

"Do you see what you do to me?" He asked in a husky voice. "What are you going to do about it?"

Ricki tilted her head back and stared up at him. "Put you back on your butt again?" She suggested.

Ristèard chuckled. "I still need to talk to you about that," he said before sobering again. "We will be leaving shortly for the planet. I need to instruct you of the dangers."

"Fine," Ricki replied. "Instruct me on the dangers, but I would like my pencil back before you do."

"For a kiss," he demanded with a savvy grin. "I will return it for a kiss."

Disappointment flashed through him when he saw the immediate wariness return to her eyes and she shook her head. Gripping the pencil in his fist, he raised his other hand and touched her hair in fascination. The more he stared at it, the more brilliant colors he saw.

"Ristèard," she whispered in a voice that was barely audible before she cleared her throat. "Grand Ruler, I believe it would be best if we keep a respectful distance between us while we try to solve the problems before you. I've been doing additional research…."

"What?" He said, shaking his head wondering what had just happened. "What research?" His eyes flickered to the tablet on the couch. "How did you get access to another device?"

Ricki pulled back and twisted out of his grasp. That was another thing that was going to have to stop. He was normally the one to dismiss a female, not the other way around.

"That isn't the point," Ricki replied with sudden excitement. "The point is I've found something that is very interesting in the archives."

"What?" He asked again, sensing a change in her as she picked up the tablet.

Ricki turned and grinned at him in triumph. Her face glowed with excitement. Even her eyes swirled with vivid blue and silver highlights that made them appear to sparkle. Caught up in her excitement, he stepped closer and looked down at the tablet in her hands.

"It's a map," she said breathlessly.

Ristèard frowned in confusion as he stared at the detailed map covered with ancient symbols. He could see it was a map, but a map to what? That was the true question. And what did all of the symbols mean?

"I can see it is a map? But, to what? How is this supposed to help Elpidios?" He asked, glancing at her before looking at the map again. "The Blood Stones…," he whispered, touching the familiar symbol still in use.

"It looks almost like a treasure map," Ricki said in a low voice. Looking up at Ristèard, she grinned. "Look here," she continued. "I think the entrance was etched on the tablets. If you turn the map this way, it matches the mountains along the edge of the Eastern desert. If we follow the coordinates it should lead us to it!"

"How did you find this?" He asked in wonder, studying the map. "How could the scientists miss it?"

Anger swept through him that such information hadn't been shared with him. If Ricki could find it, surely the scientists must have known about it. That they would ignore something of such magnitude and compound the insult by not informing him was a death sentence for treason.

"They didn't know about it," Ricki replied, biting her lip. "At least the scientists on your world wouldn't have known."

"Why?" He asked tightly, staring at her with disbelief. "If you found this within hours, why could they have not found the same thing centuries ago when they first began realizing our world was dying?"

"Because, not all of the information was found on your world," she explained. "I told you I enjoy learning about the history of other countries. I've been studying the history of Kassis. The archives are fascinating and after I figured out how to navigate through them, they were relatively easy to find the information I wanted thanks to Stan."

She rolled her eyes at him when he gave her a sharp, disapproving look when she mentioned Stan's name. That was another issue that he would need to resolve tonight. Whatever feelings she felt for the human male would need to be forgotten. Her place would be by his side after he announced it to the council.

"Go on," he said in a tight voice. "You were explaining how you found the information."

Ricki absently pushed her hair behind her ear and nodded. "I worked with Stan and Jazin to develop an algorithm to help me locate keywords. I used this type of system all the time back on Earth when I needed information. Jazin created a translation wand that when it passes over the words, it translates them for me. For any unknown words, it applies millions of different key symbols and tries to match a pattern that fits the best and makes sense. I always knew that Stan was a genius, but Jazin is pretty incredible himself," she grinned.

Ristèard was all too familiar with Jazin Ja Kel Coradon and his brother, Manota's, computer and weaponry expertise. While on Kassis, he had sent Emyr and Harald on a reconnaissance mission to gather as much information as they could find without alerting Ajaska and Torak Ja Kel Coradon. Commander Mena Rue had been right in her assessment of the advanced technology. Unfortunately, it would appear that Ajaska Ja Kel Coradon's attentions were focused on a human female now and he would not be able to use Mena Rue's previous relationship with Ajaska to find out more.

"Is it possible for anyone else to know this?" He asked, his mind swirling with what this information could mean.

If there is a treasure of Blood Stones on Elpidios, it might be enough to save it. The Blood Stones replicated quickly under the radiation of their world. The problem was, there weren't enough of them to reproduce fast enough. If there were a large stash of them, it could give them enough time for the natural process to start again.

"No, not unless they knew exactly where to look in the Kassisan archives," Ricki replied, biting her lip. "Even then, I doubt they would be able to piece it together without knowing exactly where to look. The information I found came from a collection of paintings, documents, and good, old fashioned detective work. Also, there were portions of the archives on Kassis that are not in the system and can only be accessed by the Master Librarian. The guy has been there since its inception from the look of him."

Hope built inside Ristèard as he stared down at the map. If it was genuine, it could hold Elpidios' salvation. His eyes scanned the ancient symbols. He would need someone he could trust to decipher them. He needed someone that understood how to locate information, was good at picking out the details, and could put the pieces of the puzzle together. Turning to face her, he placed his hands on Ricki's shoulders and waited for her to look up at him.

"Will you…." For a moment, his throat tightened on the unusual request. He was used to ordering people to do what he wanted. This time he would ask. "Ricki, would you be willing to help me find this treasure?"

A strange sense of expectation and nervousness filled him as he waited for her to respond. Her lips curved up into a small smile, almost as if she could sense his unfamiliar uncertainty. A relieved sigh escaped him when her hand lifted to touch his chest.

"Just try and stop me," she whispered in excitement. "Oh, Ristèard, I hope this helps your world."

Emotion choked him when she suddenly wrapped her arms around his waist and gave him a quick hug before pulling back with a nervous laugh. She shyly tucked her hair back behind her ear again and looked back down at the tablet.

At that moment, Ristèard felt as if his heart had suddenly awoken from a long sleep as another emotion welled up inside him. He knew immediately what it was… Love. He was falling in love with his unwilling Empress.

He started when the comlink at his ear chimed. They must have arrived at the Spaceport and the transport was ready for their departure. Tapping it impatiently, he waited for Andras to respond.

"Is the transport ready?" He asked, staring at Ricki's sun-kissed hair.

"Yes," Andras responded in a clipped tone. "Be prepared for a welcoming committee. Manderlin informed the council that you had returned with the Empress of Elpidios."

Chapter 12

Ricki nodded as Ristèard, Emyr, and Sadao all gave her instructions. Her brow creased with concern. She had never been in such a dangerous situation before. One thing she wasn't about to do was discount what they were telling her. She could tell from the intensity of their expressions and the worry in their eyes that they meant what they were saying.

"What should you do at all times?" Ristèard asked.

Ricki nervously smiled. "Always keep Sadao and Emyr on each side of me. Harald will protect my back. If anything should happen, I will follow Sadao. He will keep me safe until you and the others can come … or," her throat tightened for a moment, making it difficult to speak. "Or until Ajaska or Torak are alerted. Did you talk to my father yet? Does he know that I'm safe? Well, sort of safe, only don't tell him the 'sort of' part. Dad is very protective of me and mom."

She saw the flash of unease cross Ristèard's face. Worry gnawed at her when she saw him look away. Reaching out, she touched his arm.

"You didn't tell them, did you?" She asked in a quiet voice.

Ristèard shifted in his seat. The transport was much smaller than she had imagined it would be. This one contained six passenger seats bolted at the floor and ceiling. Three of them were on one side and faced the three opposing ones on the other side. Sadao and Emyr each took a seat on either side of her while Ristèard sat directly across from her. Andras and Harald were piloting the transport down to the planet.

"Ajaska and I spoke," he replied in a gruff tone. "He is aware that I took you."

Ricki raised her eyebrow at him. From the way he squirmed a little in his seat, there were a few details that he had neglected to share with her. If he wanted her help, he was going to have to learn that she liked to have all the details, not just what he felt like sharing.

"And… What was his response? Did you tell him why you took me?" Ricki paused and frowned at that. "Why did you take me? I know you think I look like this Empress of Elpidios, but I can assure you that I'm not. I seriously doubt your people even knew about humans or Earth back then."

Except for that one reference that still didn't make any sense, she thought.

Star had told her about a dream she had and it matched one of the stories in the archive. Ricki had dismissed it as just a dream, but now, she couldn't help but wonder. What if it was true and somehow, someway, the people of Earth had once traveled the stars?

She blinked when Ristèard suddenly leaned forward as far as the straps across his chest and lap would let him. The fierce look in his gaze made her swallow nervously. She had a feeling she wasn't going to like what he was about to tell her.

"It doesn't matter what I believe or not," he replied in a low, intense tone. "What matters is what my people think. If they believe you are the prophesied Empress of Elpidios that has returned to save their world, then you are. Time is running out for my world, Ricki. If the information you have found proves to be unsuccessful, hundreds of millions of Elpidiosians will perish. I took you because I needed you. That is the only reason you need to understand. You are a symbol of hope for my people. Ajaska is aware that you are here and I have given my word that I would keep you safe. He will inform your parents. There is nothing he or your father can do about that now."

Ricki schooled her face to hide the hurt she felt at his words. He was right. Just because they had shared a few kisses didn't mean anything. She needed to focus on her original plan, help Ristèard and his people if she could and return to Kassis and her own family. Once she returned, she would see if Stan was interested in trying a second date.

"Very well," she replied coolly. "Once we are down on your planet, I would like to have full access to any information you might have pertaining to the history of your world. This should include both digital and hard copy materials."

Ristèard leaned back with a nod. "We will meet with the council first. Afterwards, I will give you what access you don't already have," he stated dryly. "Once I am free, I will give you a tour of the palace."

"Thank you," Ricki said, sitting back in her seat when the transport bounced. "I look forward to learning more about the history of your world."

He nodded his head in acknowledgement before turning his attention to the two men sitting on either side of her. She distractedly listened as Emyr, Sadao, and Ristèard discussed what they expected to happen at the council meeting. Her mind turned to the material she had found so far.

Glancing down, she opened the tablet in her hands back to the map. She studied it carefully, enlarging sections of it so that she could see the symbols marked on it better. Opening her purse, she pulled the thin scanner Jazin had given her out and ran it over the corner of map at some symbols that were very faint.

Frustration swept through her. She really wished she had the actual, physical map in her hands. If it was still in existence, she would find it. Her hand slid down the smooth glass when the transport turned as it began banking for landing. The scanner light flashed as it passed over a section of the map that looked blank.

Ricki glanced under her eyelashes at Ristèard. He was busy talking still. Lowering her eyes to the slate in her hand, she ran it carefully back over the screen. It took several tries before the scanner picked up the almost invisible symbols. Narrowing her eyes, she waited for the scanner to decipher the words.

Careful seeker for the treasure lies protected by the guardians of Elpidios. Only those true of heart led by one born with blood of ice can pass through the crystal doors. Keep a wary eye, for dangers lurk to keep safe the treasure that will heal this world. Emera

"Who is Emera?" Ricki asked, looking up at Ristèard.

All three men stopped talking and only the sound of the engines of the transport could be heard for several long seconds. From the look of surprise in Ristèard's eyes, it was a name that meant something to him. Pushing her glasses back up on her nose, she waited for his response.

"She was the first Empress," he stated with a shrug. "It was said she was crazy, but she is the one who ordered the building of the underground cities that would later save the people of Elpidios. It is believed that she was not from our world, but that the First Emperor fell under the spell she cast and claimed her as his bride. Legend states she died during the birth of their second son."

"Why are you called the Grand Ruler if the previous rulers were called Emperor?" Ricki asked, looking back and forth. "I apologize for not having more knowledge, but I wasn't expecting to be kidnapped. If I had known, I would have brushed up on your history."

Both Sadao and Emyr chuckled at her pointed reference. Ristèard shot both men a dark look before he returned his gaze to her. A frown creased his brow and he sat back in his seat and folded his arms across his chest.

"My father changed the name to Grand Ruler and redesigned the council appointments to elected positions," he informed her.

"After we killed the others," Emyr chuckled. "The former council was made up of warlords from the different zones that cared nothing for their people, just for the power and wealth they could amass on the backs of their subjects."

"That power and wealth came from the Blood Crystals that they sold for weapons to off-worlders," Sadao added quietly. "When Ristèard's grandfather tried to stop them, they turned on him."

Ristèard nodded. "My father was imprisoned," he told her in a grim voice. "What they did not expect was that he would build a resistance among the prisoners."

"That included our parents," Emyr added. "Our bond is the fact that each of us was born in the bowels of an Elpidios prison."

Ricki glanced at each of the men in horror. "Each of you… How?" She asked in shock.

Ristèard shook his head. "It doesn't matter. Emera was the first Empress. She was considered crazy and banned to the deserts of Elpidios to live out her final days as an outcast," he said. "We are landing, remember what we told you."

Ricki nodded. She was too stunned by the information she had learned to ask any more questions at the moment. There was so much she didn't understand, but wanted to know.

She silently studied the man across from her. He stared back at her in silence, daring her to feel pity for him. Pity was the last emotion she felt; Respect, confusion, and understanding, yes. Pity? Never. Ristèard Roald was a man used to violence, a life on the edge and he was perfectly capable of handling both.

Ricki pulled her gaze away from him to look out the front window. Her throat tightened as she caught her first glance at the capital city of Elpidios. A huge, black palace rose high above the city that surrounded it. It looked as if it had been carved into the mountain where it stood like a magnificent sentinel watching over the citizens far below.

"Welcome to my world, Ricki Bailey," Ristèard murmured as the transport began its descent.

Chapter 13

Ristèard discreetly watched Ricki's face, trying to decipher what her reaction would be to his home before he turned to press the control to open the loading platform. He nodded to Andras when his second-in-command murmured that he had checked with the elite guards at the palace and made sure that everything was secured for his and Ricki's arrival. His mouth tightened when the loading ramp to the transport lowered and he saw the crowd pushing against the guards.

Ricki stepped up next to him and stared in shock at the crowd. Her fingers nervously twisted the end of the braid she had quickly weaved to keep her hair out of her face. A loud roar sounded from the crowd when they caught sight of them.

"They appear to be very happy to see you," she murmured, gazing with wide eyes at the large crowd.

Ristèard's mouth tightened into a straight line. "It is not me they are here to see," he responded, placing his hand on the small of her back. "It is you."

Ricki's head jerked around to stare at him in disbelief. She stumbled a little on the edge of the platform as he guided her down it. He quickly wrapped his arm around her waist to steady her. A low chanting began in the background, slowly rising by the time they reached the end of the platform.

"Why?" She asked, gazing around at the thousands of blue skinned people staring at her. "Why would they come to see me?"

Ristèard slipped his hand from around her waist and threaded his fingers through hers. Raising their entwined hands up above their heads, he stared down at the huge crowd of people. A wave of hopeful cries rose like a wave. The sound crashed around them as his people acknowledged that the rumor of the mythical Empress of Elpidios was true. She had returned to save them.

"You are their Empress," he whispered in her ear. "You have returned to save Elpidios."

Ricki felt her knees grow weak and her head swam for a moment. Ristèard felt her sway. He did the only thing he could think of to keep her from fainting. Lowering their entwined hands, he turned her toward him and wrapped his other arm around her.

"Ristèard?" Ricki whispered, her eyes glazed and disoriented. "What if...?"

Ristèard didn't wait for her to finish her sentence. Pulling her roughly against his body, he captured her lips with his. He blocked the loud roar of approval from the crowds. His only focus was on Ricki right now. This was not the way he would have liked to have introduced her to his world, but he could reluctantly appreciate Manderlin's move. There would be no denying Ricki's existence to his people now.

Pride seared through him when he felt her body shudder and relax for a moment before she broke their kiss. She blinked several times and he saw her vision clear as she looked up at him. His hand rose to cup her soft cheek.

"I'm sorry," he whispered, staring down at her with regret. "This is not how I wanted to introduce you to my world."

A faint, reluctant smile curved Ricki's lips and she shook her head at him. "You should have thought about that before you kidnapped me," she teased in a faint voice before glancing at the suddenly quiet crowd. "I'm terrified I'll let them down," she admitted, turning away from him and smiling down at a group of young children peering through the legs of the guards.

"You aren't the only one," Ristèard muttered under his breath, watching as Ricki walked down the steps of the landing platform and crossed over to where the children were watching her with awe. "You aren't the only one," he repeated before he followed her.

* * *

"Take her to my rooms," Ristèard ordered quietly to Sadao an hour later. "Stay with her and keep her safe. And Sadao, do not trust anyone."

"Of course," Sadao replied, bowing his head at Ristèard and resting his hand over his heart to show his respect and allegiance. "Lady Ricki."

Ristèard saw Ricki hesitate for a fraction of a second, her worried gaze focused on him before she nodded. Another wave of pride swept through him when she ignored the harsh shouts directed at her. She had stood by his side, her head held high, listening to and observing the fury that had burst from several of the councilmen. He had been right when he said that having Ricki beside him would show the true colors of those that opposed him.

Fury burned through him as the circle of men on either side of him continued to argue with each other. The threats were growing louder, and he suspected that it would turn to violence before too much longer. He was positive his next move would push the traitors out into the open.

"Enough!" He roared, bringing instant silence to the room. "You have defied me for the last time. As of now, the council is dissolved. Those that wish to challenge my right to do so stand before me now and we will deal with this once and for all."

Ristèard's face twisted in disgust as Texla and Roamlin both rose from their seats and pulled their weapons. It would appear the puppets wanted to play. His eyes narrowed when five other councilmen rose and jumped over the sides of the circular room to land in the center. Only three councilmen remained seated, Manderlin, Pertilis, and Dertus.

"We have been trying to kill you for years, Prison rat," Texla snarled. "But, you and your fellow rodents have continued to slip through the traps we have set. No longer will that happen."

Ristèard glanced at Andras, who moved closer so that he was standing back to back with Ristèard. He knew that Harald and Emyr were also in the room. Each of his trusted personal guards, and the only men he would call friends, had taken up a position in the room. Seven against four wasn't bad odds. He could handle that many on his own.

He turned his head, watching as one of the guards at the door slipped through it before the other guard locked it behind him.

Six other guards slipped in through the back entrance to the council room.

Okay, fourteen to four, he thought with grim determination.

"Who pulls your strings, Texla?" Ristèard mocked, sliding the blades at his waist out and extending them. "I was told you are just the puppet. There is always a master because the puppet is too dumb to move on his own."

Texla hissed and sneered back at Ristèard. "I am no puppet," he snarled. "The wealth I have collected will keep me comfortable for the rest of my life."

Ristèard's face froze into a cold, deadly mask. "You would sell your planet for your own personal gains, but you will not live long enough to collect on it," he promised. "I will see you and every other traitor to Elpidios dead first."

Texla chuckled. "You are outnumbered, Grand Ruler," he sneered, waving the blade in his hand toward the guards circling the center area. "Two against all of us, this time you are the one who will finally be dead. You and that female you brought to

Elpidios. Even as you stand here, our men are on their way to kill her."

"Not just two," Manderlin roared, rising up and striking at one of the guards closest to him. "Five!"

"Kill them all!" Texla ordered, stepping in to attack Ristèard. "Kill them!"

* * *

Ricki glanced at Sadao with a worried look. She knew that they had discussed this might happen, but that didn't make it any easier. She started to glance back over her shoulder, but Sadao stopped her.

"Do not look back," he murmured in a quiet voice, raising his hand to grip her arm and picking up the pace of their walk. "We are being followed."

Ricki nodded. Glancing back and forth, she didn't have much time to enjoy the beauty of the palace. The walls of the palace were so smooth that the surface resembled a highly polished mirror. The only light coming into the long corridor was either from the large windows they passed by or from hidden lights along the walls.

Ricki reached her hand out to touch the surface as they turned the corner. A gasped escaped her when threads of gold blossomed from where her fingers touched it.

"The stone contains a natural chemical that reacts to touch," Sadao explained in a quiet voice as they neared a narrow staircase. "Do not touch it until we get to safety."

Ricki nodded again, pulling her hand back and wrapping her fingers around the strap of her purse.

She was thankful she seldom wore heels. The soft, yellow dress shoes that she was wearing were not only comfortable, but quiet against the tiled floor.

She quickly followed Sadao up the stairs and down several more corridors before they halted in front of a set of huge, ornately carved black doors guarded by two men. Sadao muttered to them in a low tone that they were being followed and to be prepared. Both men nodded and quickly pulled one door open to allow them passage.

Ricki nervously glanced over her shoulder when she heard the sound of footsteps coming down the corridor. Jumping slightly when she felt a hand on her arm, she turned to look at Sadao with wide, frightened eyes. He gave her a reassuring smile before he nodded toward the opening.

"Go," he said, glancing over his shoulder.

Ricki quickly slipped through the door. Sadao followed her, locking it behind him. Turning, she gazed at what appeared to be an elaborate office. Her eyes moved about the room.

Huge tapestries depicting different events covered the mirrored black walls. She walked around the room, glancing nervously back at the door. They were so thick, she doubted they would hear anything on the other side of them. Sadao moved to the desk and began pressing a series of buttons. Within seconds, heavy shields came down over the large windows and lights came on.

"I need to make sure the rest of the rooms are secure," Sadao said, rising from the chair. "There are two other rooms connected to this one. Stay here."

"What about the guards outside?" Ricki asked, worriedly glancing at the door. "You can't let them face whoever is coming alone."

"They are well trained and additional guards have been alerted. Ristèard ordered that I remain with you. Trust me, I would fear him far more than the traitors," Sadao stated. "I will return in a moment."

Ricki swallowed her protest. She turned in a slow circle, gazing around the room. A fireplace large enough for her to stand in covered most of the far wall. Several large logs, twice as thick as her body and just as long as she was tall, burned in it.

Over the mantle of the fireplace was a tapestry of two men. They stood side by side, a look of fierce determination on their bloodied faces. Ricki stepped closer to look carefully at the men. One man was slightly older than the other. It took a moment for Ricki to realize that the younger man was Ristèard. In the picture, they held a bloody sword and were surrounded by the remains of dozens of dead men.

Fascination and nausea coursed through her as she studied the surrounding area in the image. The more she looked, the more details began to emerge. In the background, she could pick out the images of Emyr, Andras, Harald, and Sadao, along with dozens of other men, women, and children. Some of them were still imprisoned behind large bars. It was an image of a woman, holding the small, lifeless body of a child in her arms that pulled at Ricki.

Her eyes went back to the two men standing surrounded by the dead. The older man's eyes held so much emotion in them, so much heartbreak, she could actually feel his pain.

Turning away from the tapestry, she looked at the sealed windows that graced the west wall. They covered the wall from floor to ceiling, probably to allow the greatest amount of natural lighting into the room. Heavy curtains outlined each window and were pulled back with thick ropes of silver and gold.

Ricki continued her exploration. A large round table that could seat at least a dozen men sat near the center of the room. Two large, silver couches with twin matching chairs were arranged in front of the burning fireplace. There were six matching end tables made of the same black stone as the walls. They sat at the end of each piece of furniture.

Curious, she walked over and touched one. Amazement swept through her when she saw spider webs of gold filament light up through the stone before fading again. It was almost magical.

Wrapping her arms back around her waist, she walked over to one of the tapestries hanging along the wall behind the large desk. It had to be over fifteen feet tall and twenty feet wide.

There was a picture of what looked almost like a maze on it. Inside the maze were depictions of different scenes. Stepping closer, she knelt down to study the bottom of the tapestry where it almost touched the floor. Her fingers instinctively reached out to touch the figure of the woman woven into it.

A wave of dizziness swept through Ricki for a moment as she bent down. She thought it might have been because she hadn't eaten in over twenty-four hours. Closing her eyes, she pressed her hand against the tapestry to keep her balance. The wave of dizziness continued to increase until she knew that she was going to faint.

It was strange being able to analyze what was happening to her even as she felt her body shifting sideways until she was lying on the floor between the desk and the wall. She tried to open her eyes, but it was useless. Instead, she allowed the darkness to take her. Something deep inside her told her that this was important. She sank further down into the swirling mist as vivid colors exploded behind her eyelids.

I wonder if this is what Star saw when she had her dream, Ricki thought as she gave in to the brilliant lights.

* * *

Ristèard struck Texla hard across the face as the man came at him again. The blow knocked the traitorous bastard into Roamlin. Swinging his blade low, he caught Roamlin across the stomach when Texla jerked the man in front of him as protection. The blade sliced Roamlin's stomach from one side to the other.

He ignored the choked scream of the dying man, instead turning to stop one of Texla's guards from running him through from behind. Swinging both blades with a cold precision, he dispatched the guard and turned back to find Texla. He wanted answers and the greedy bastard was going to provide them for him before he died.

"Ristèard, behind you," Emyr shouted, twisting in an effort to get away from the two guards attacking him.

Ristèard sidestepped and turned on his heel, bowing low. The blade aimed for his neck swished over his head by the width of his little finger. Thrusting forward, he buried the short sword in his left hand into the chest of the guard. He yanked the sword out and turned as another guard came at him.

"Harald, try to get to Ricki and Sadao," he shouted, his eyes scanning over the fighting mass, searching for Texla. "Texla!" He roared, spying the sneaky bastard climbing over the body of one of the elderly councilmen.

Texla turned and sneered. The sneer turned to panic when the door to the council room exploded inward. His eyes widened when he saw an assortment of unusual men standing in the doorway.

He immediately recognized the Kassisan, but not the others with him. The two large men standing on either side of two smaller beings, suddenly shuddered. As they did, their bodies began to contort and change into massive creatures with thick, silvery scales.

"Kill them," Texla yelled in a shrilled voice. "Kill them!"

Ristèard's face twisted in rage at the cowardly traitor's retreat. "I think not. Ajaska, find Ricki! She is in danger," he yelled, climbing over the low wall that led to the upper sitting area.

"I will go," Jarmen replied, his eyes glowing a dark red. "She is in his office, according to the current video surveillance."

"Marvin, take Walter and Nema to safety," Ajaska ordered, striking at several men as they attacked.

A low snarl behind Ristèard had him twisting. He found himself face to face with one of the Kor d'lur. The man's eyes swept upward. The large creature grabbed one of the chairs next to him and swung it at Texla, catching the man in the back with a satisfied snort.

"Thanks," Ristèard grunted, jumping up onto the table and using them as stairs to get to the fallen man. Dropping down next to Texla, he rolled the man over onto his back and struck him hard across the jaw. "Now, I'll show you how a Prison rat makes someone talk," he growled, running the tip of his sword along Texla's stomach.

"Ristèard!" Andras called out urgently.

Ristèard shifted, glancing at Andras, who was climbing up the side of the platform. The look of worry in his second-in-commands eyes told him that something had happened. His eyes flickered around the room.

He could see that Ajaska and the Kor d'lur were finishing up the remaining rebels while Emyr was pressing a cloth to Manderlin's shoulder. His gaze moved back down to Texla. The male was still dazed from the blow from the chair and from where he had hit him.

"Ristèard, Sadao just contacted me," Andras said in a low voice. "Ricki collapsed. Sadao says he cannot get her to wake."

Fear burst through Ristèard. Bending, he pulled Texla up by the front of his shirt and struck him hard across the jaw with the butt of his sword. Texla's head fell backwards from the blow. Ristèard dropped the man and twisted.

"Make sure he and any of his men that are still alive are locked up," Ristèard snarled, jumping down onto the lower floor of the council room. "And Andras, make sure all the traitors are cleared from the palace. Keep only those that you trust within its walls."

He didn't wait for any of the others. His mind was on Ricki. He would kill Sadao if he let anything happen to her. Fear drove him through the corridors. He slowed briefly when he saw the litter of bodies on the floor.

Ristèard slowed when he noticed Jarmen kneeling outside of his office door, attending to one of the wounded guards. The unusual male glanced up briefly, his eyes glowing an eerie red for a moment before they changed to black when he recognized Ristèard. Ignoring Jarmen, he touched the panel near the door with his hand.

The moment the locks disengaged, he pulled the massive door open and stepped inside, his eyes immediately searching for Ricki's golden hair and slender body. He saw Sadao rise up from behind his desk. Worry and concern creased his brow as he returned Ristèard's questioning gaze.

"I only left her for a few moments to check that the other rooms were secured. When I returned, I found her lying here," Sadao explained, moving out of the way when Ristèard strode forward. "Her breathing appears normal and I cannot find any signs of trauma. I've tried to wake her, but she doesn't respond. It is as if she is in some type of trance."

..*.

Ricki turned in a circle, trying to figure out where she was. A gasp escaped her when she saw the figure of a woman striding toward her. The woman looked just like her! She staggered backwards when the figure walked right through her body.

Turning in disbelief, Ricki watched as the woman glanced back toward her with a frown before turning and disappearing around the corner. Curious, Ricki followed her. Surprise and fascination filled her when she saw that the long corridor she had been standing in was actually the entrance to a large, underground city.

Glancing back the way she came, she saw the mammoth sized doors at the far end. The corridor was actually a bridge that led from the doors to the city. On each side of the bridge was a vast crevice. Ricki couldn't see anything in the inky blackness below the bridge. She had no idea how deep it was.

Something told her that she really didn't want to find out.

Returning her gaze back to the entrance, she scanned the crowded steps for the woman. It wasn't hard to find the fair complexion and white-blonde hair among all the shadowy figures of black-haired and blue-skinned men and women surrounding her. She thought it was strange that only the woman appeared clearly defined. All the other figures held a ghostly appearance in contrast.

Ricki noticed that the woman appeared to be talking urgently to several of the men. She continued to stare at the woman, curious about who she was and why she was there. It wasn't until the woman turned sideways to argue with a tall, stately man that Ricki realized that the woman was very pregnant.

Ricki twisted back and forth as more figures hurried by her. She followed them as they rushed up to the small group on the steps. As she drew closer, she caught the hushed words between the woman and the man.

"Emera, it is too dangerous," the man insisted. "Let one of the others finish the task."

The woman shook her head. "You know that I am the only one who can seal the last door, my Emperor. It has to be checked," Emera replied with a tired smile. "You must convince your people to move to the underground cities before the creatures I warned you about come to your world. You must tell them the radiation outside is growing too dangerous for them to continue to live upon the surface. Please, the creatures destroyed the world of my father's people, do not let them destroy yours as well."

The ghostly figure of the Emperor raised his hand and stroked Emera's cheek. She turned her face into his hand and pressed a kiss to his palm. Ricki's heart melted at the tender touch. She could feel the grief and helplessness of the couple.

"Go then," he ordered in a hard voice. "Take two of the warriors with you. Seal the chamber and set the traps. The creatures must not be able to reach it. And Emera, be safe."

"I will," Emera whispered, pulling away. "Hurry, I fear there is not much time left."

Ricki jerked as Emera and two men ran through her and back up the steps. She turned to follow, but felt as if she was falling. A low cry escaped her as the world around her spun dizzily in a circle of mist.

Flashes of images flooded her mind. It was as if she was trapped in the tapestry and going through the maze alongside Emera. Shadowy images rose up, solidified, then faded away again as the ancient Empress of Elpidios carefully guided the two men with her past the traps they encountered along the way.

Emera finally stumbled to a halt in front of a set of huge doors. Tears glistened in her eyes as she stared up at the intricately carved entrance. One of the men stepped forward and grabbed Emera when she started to collapse. After several seconds, she spoke quietly to the man and he reluctantly released her.

The two men stepped back several feet as Emera lifted her hands and placed them on the door. Amazement gripped Ricki as thin lines of frost moved up the beautiful black stone doors. The carving reminded Ricki of the one on the door to the office, only on a much larger scale. Ice crystals formed, outlining an image set in the very center. It was only when the ice touched the center that a set of circular forms detached from each other and began turning. As they did, the massive doors slowly opened.

"I need to see it one last time," Emera whispered. "You must protect it from falling into the wrong hands. It has the power to save your people. The creatures will do everything they can, to get it back. You must not allow that to happen."

The two shadowy guards nodded. Ricki turned her head to see what Emera was talking about, but the sounds of loud voices broke through her dream, pulling her back to consciousness. She fought to see inside the area before the doors sealed again, but the voices, combined with the sudden feeling of floating on a hard cloud, drew her too far to the surface.

"I'll roast your balls and feed them to Katarina's cats," a very familiar voice threatened. "When I'm done with that, I'll feed the rest of you to them."

Ricki fought to open her eyes. Fear and confusion swamped her when the first thing she saw was Ristèard's blood-soaked face. Her hand rose and touched his chin, freezing when he suddenly stopped and looked down at her with worried eyes.

"Lay her on the couch," a soft voice insisted. "I'll take care of her while you teach him a lesson, Walter."

"Mom," Ricki whispered, blinking again to clear her vision. She turned her head and saw her mother standing by the couch. "What are you doing here?"

"I'll tell you what we are doing here," her father growled in a low, menacing voice. "We are taking you home before this... this criminal gets you killed, is what we are doing here."

"She is not going anywhere," Ristèard snapped as he carefully lowered Ricki onto the couch. "Emyr, check her over. Sadao, what happened? I warned you to keep her safe."

Ricki's head swiveled back and forth to the different people in the room. Ristèard, Andras, Emyr, and Harald looked like they had taken a bath in a slaughter house. She blinked when she saw Ajaska and Jazin's friend, Jarmen, standing in the corner conversing with Marvin and Martin.

"No, Ricki. Just lay there, sweetheart, while I make sure you are alright," her mom was saying in a soft, concerned voice when Ricki struggled to sit up. "How many fingers am I holding up?"

Ricki rolled her eyes. That was the first question her mom always asked, whether she had a cut, skinned knee, head cold, or the flu. Her mother was very good at many things, but medicine was not one of them.

"Two, mom," Ricki replied impatiently as she slid her legs off the couch and sat up. "You always hold up two fingers."

Nema patted Ricki on her knee. "You'll be fine," she sighed in relief.

Ricki's eyes slid past everyone to the tapestry hanging on the wall behind the desk. It suddenly made complete sense. The map led them to the location of the entrance where the 'treasure of Elpidios' was hidden, but the tapestry told them how to get it. Rising off the couch, she ignored her mom and dad's protests.

She moved forward, mesmerized by the information she was seeing. Her eyes roamed the maze, picking out the key symbols, translating them with what she already knew, and continued. She didn't stop until she had reached the end of the labyrinth of corridors and the picture of Emera standing in front of the great doors that held the key to Elpidios' salvation.

Strong arms wrapped around her when she swayed. Blinking, she looked up into Ristèard's dark silver eyes with sudden understanding. She didn't need to search the archives for the answers, they were right here. His ancestors had the answer to their salvation right in front of them all this time and didn't even realize it.

Ricki's eyes returned to the tapestry as the room became deathly quiet. She tilted her head as she stared at the figure of the woman in the center. A frown creased her brow as she tried to figure out the last piece to the puzzle.

Only those true of heart led by one born with blood of ice can pass through the crystal doors.

Blood of ice, she thought, slowly raising her hands up in front of her as she thought of Emera doing the same thing in her dream.

Loud gasps echoed through the room when frosty, icy crystals formed over her slender fingers, rising up to form spirals in the air before turning to mist.

"Who am I? What am I?" She asked in a small, whispered voice filled with fear and confusion. She turned to look at her parents with pleading eyes. "Mom, where did I come from?"

Chapter 14

Later that evening, Ristèard watched Ricki from across the room, unable to pull his gaze away from her pale face. She smiled at her father when he reached over and took the empty plate she was holding, out of her hands. He had immediately ordered a meal for her, feeling a sense of remorse that he hadn't thought of it earlier.

A part of him wanted to order everyone out of his office. Everyone, that is, but Ricki. A primitive part of him wanted to be alone with her and he resented having to share her attentions, even with her parents, which confused him even more.

"They are confusing, aren't they?" Ajaska asked, holding out a glass of liquor.

Ristèard absently nodded as he took the offered drink. Downing it in one swallow, he held it out for more. He ignored Ajaska's chuckle as the smart-ass Kassisan Ambassador poured more of the dark green liquid into his glass.

"Who is she?" Ristèard asked, raising the small chalice of potent liquor to his lips again.

"If I had to guess, I would say she is part Glacian. I've met their Ambassador a few times. Her eyes are the same color as his. Their star system just recently joined the Alliance council. They are a tough bunch of bastards. They are ruled by a Coalition with a group of directors. Ambassador Rime was recently appointed as a representative to the Alliance," Ajaska commented, studying Ricki with a frown. "What I would like to know is how in the hell a Glacian ended up on Earth and no one knew about it."

"Probably the same way the Kor d'lurs did," Ristèard muttered, staring at where Marvin and Martin stood in silence. "I think they may know more than they are letting on."

* * *

Ajaska looked at Ristèard in surprise before he turned his attention back to the two tall, silent men standing near the fireplace. They had refused to remain behind on Kassis when he had stated his plans to kidnap Ricki back. His first thought had been because they were so protective of Walter and Nema, now he wondered if it had more to do with Ricki.

He glanced over to where Jarmen was standing in front of the window looking down over the city, or appeared to be looking down over it. Jarmen was, in fact, hacking into Ristèard's computer system. Taking a sip of his drink, Ajaska gazed to where Ricki was quietly talking to her parents. Nema sat next to her daughter, tightly holding Ricki's slender hand in her smaller one.

"I should… Thank you for your assistance earlier," Ristèard suddenly said, draining his drink after the unusual words.

"But," Ajaska prompted.

Ristèard glanced at Ajaska's amused face. "But, I want you to know that Ricki will not be returning to Kassis with you."

Ajaska leaned back against the wall next to him and studied Ristèard. The man was not much older than Jazin. In many ways, he saw the same types of characteristics in Ristèard that he saw in his own sons.

He could see the pride, fierce determination, and the need to feel complete in the Grand Ruler that he saw in his sons before they found their mates. He reluctantly admitted, he felt the same way himself as the image of a dark-haired Russian beauty formed in his mind.

Ajaska doubted that Ristèard was even aware that every time he looked at Ricki, his face softened and his eyes lost the hard, cold distance or that his face softened with... love. The Grand Ruler of Elpidios was in love with the delicate half human/half Glacian woman he had kidnapped.

* * *

It was well after midnight by the time everyone finally called it a night. Ristèard had ordered one of the guards at the door to escort her and her parents to the living quarters where they would be staying. He assured them that those that remained in the palace were loyal only to him when her dad grumbled that he would prefer to return to Ajaska's warship with her and her mom.

Ristèard had stubbornly refused her dad's request. It wasn't until he threatened to send her parents back alone, that her dad reluctantly agreed to spend one night here. Ricki knew her dad was just trying to be protective of her and her mom, but he also understood the importance of helping to save an entire planet of people.

The guard had shown her to one set of rooms while her parents had been given the quarters across the hallway. The quarters were elegantly decorated, but in a slightly masculine theme. The thick, black walls shimmered with the threads of gold, illuminating the large living area.

A long, plush black and gold couch and two matching chairs were placed before the fireplace. Just like in the office, it was large enough for her to stand in. A low fire burned in it, heating the room to a comfortable level. Her eyes tiredly swept over the room. So much had happened over the last few days that she felt like she had run a marathon.

Deciding her exploration of the rooms could wait until the next day when she wasn't so exhausted, she decided to find the closest bed and crash. Turning on the woven carpet covering the polished black floors, she walked down the long hallway. She noticed that several of the doors were closed while one was left open.

Ricki paused in the entrance to the massive bedroom. In the center was a large bed. From the ceiling, thick curtains hung down around it. They were tied back at the moment and the covers of the bed were turned down, as if to invite a willing occupant to climb in and rest.

Her eyes lit on the long, blue nightgown and robe that were laid out across the foot of the bed. Relief washed through her. Crossing over to the bed, she picked up the beautiful, blue silk material. It actually shimmered in the low light of the room.

She glanced around again, looking to see if there was a bathroom in the room or if it was detached. A sigh of relief escaped her when she saw the lit room to the side. Deciding that a nice hot shower would definitely help her sleep, she grabbed the matching robe off the bed and disappeared into the bathroom.

A short time later, a clean and relaxed Ricki sat on the small bench, brushing her hair and thinking about everything that had happened earlier in the day. From what she had discovered, Ajaska, Jarmen, Marvin, Martin, and her parents had arrived just as the coup d'état started. Ajaska and Jarmen had heard the sound of fighting in the council room and burst through the doors.

Glancing at her hands, she set the brush she was using down on the vanity table in front of her. Lifting her right hand, she thought about what had happened earlier in Ristèard's office. Focusing, she thought of Emera again and the ice coming from the ancient Empress' hands.

A shiver escaped Ricki when she saw tiny crystals forming on the tips of her fingers. The more she concentrated, the more the ice formed until she had a small spear protruding from the ends. Her hand froze suddenly as the door behind her opened. A surprised gasp parted her lips when she saw Ristèard's reflection in the mirror of the vanity. He silently stood in the doorway, staring back at her with an intensity that shook her.

"You shouldn't be here," she murmured in a husky voice, clenching her fist as the icy blade dissolved into a mist. She turned on the small seat until she was facing him. Rising from the padded bench, she self-consciously raised a hand to pull the robe close over the low neckline of the nightgown. "Is everything alright?"

Her worried eyes flashed over him. His hair was damp, as if he also had just showered, and he wore only a pair of soft pants that hung low on his hips. She tried not to stare at his body, but it was impossible with him wearing so little.

His body was like sculptured marble, smooth, taut, yet so soft looking that it made her want to run her hands over it. The blue color of his skin appeared to shimmer with silver, almost the way the black stone of the palace rippled with gold when she ran her fingers across it. A part of her wondered if she touched him, if the silver threads would dance across his skin.

She drew in a breath when he nodded and stepped into the room. Her body felt like someone had lit a torch inside it. She chided herself for thinking such outrageous thoughts when it was obvious he was exhausted and had probably just come to make sure she was alright after her earlier collapse. Giving herself a mental kick in the butt, she forced herself to focus on the reason he was there and not his body.

"As right as it can be at the moment," he replied in a weary voice. "The council has been dissolved."

"That tends to happen when you kill most of them," she replied, dryly. "What are your plans now?"

"I have sent Harald and Emyr to take control of the zones until a replacement for each one can be made," he said, pausing when he was just a few steps from her. "They may not be necessary if a solution isn't found soon. Ajaska has assigned Jarmen to look at the current shields and see if anything can be done. He has also brought another supply of crystals."

"What are you not telling me?" Ricki asked, tilting her head. "I can see it in your eyes. Something is wrong."

"The crystals the Kassisans have are breaking down much faster than we anticipated," he murmured. "There is no way they can keep up with the demand, even if they tripled their production."

"Why? I thought the crystals were the same?" Ricki asked, confused.

"So did we, until further analysis," Ristèard admitted. "They are close, but the oxide materials are slightly different. The metal is unlike anything we have seen before, and not found naturally on either planet."

"Alien," Ricki murmured, thinking of the vault in her dream. "Emera said she wanted to see it one more time."

"Emera?" Ristèard asked, puzzled.

Ricki released a nervous chuckle and tucked her hair behind her ear. "When I was unconscious, I was dreaming about Emera," she confessed. "I swore it felt like I was there. Star had a similar dream. I know I just fainted due to low blood sugar, but everything seemed so real. Emera went to the maze that was on the tapestry hanging on the wall. At the end of it is a set of huge doors with the same engravings that are on the door to your office, but on a much larger scale. I think your ancestors knew that the best place to keep the key to the maze was right in front of everyone."

"What was in the vault?" Ristèard asked with a frown. "Is it the Blood Stones?"

Ricki shook her head in regret. "I don't know," she whispered. "Like most dreams, I woke up before I could see what was inside. In the morning, I want to take a closer look at both the tapestry and the doors," she added. "I think that is where we might find the answers you are seeking."

Ristèard stared down into her eyes, losing himself in them. He followed her slender fingers as she tucked her hair behind her ear again. Reaching out, he touched the silky, white-gold strands. Unable to resist, he slid his fingers through the silky waves until he cupped the back of her head, pulling her gently toward him.

"Ristèard," she whispered, sliding her hands up between them.

He paused, but didn't let her go. "One kiss," he murmured. "I want to know."

Ricki's eyes darkened at the deep, rough emotion in his voice. "What do you want to know?" She asked, relaxing her hands and splaying her fingers across his bare chest.

"If the fire is still there," he whispered before he captured her lips with his.

Ricki could have told him the fire was not only there, it was bloody out of control whenever he touched her. The cool façade she tried to hide behind evaporated just like the ice from her fingers.

For once, she didn't even think about analyzing the kiss. She didn't think about whether the man kissing her would be a good fit for her. All she could think of was how great it felt and the feel of his hands on her body.

A long sigh escaped her when he continued to kiss her. Sliding her hands up his chest, she wound them around his neck so she could press herself closer. She didn't understand why, but everything about this felt... right.

She moaned when he broke the kiss to run his lips down along her jaw to her throat. Tilting her head to the side, she shivered at the warm, moist touch of his lips against her sensitive skin. Her right hand curled around the back of his head, pressing him closer to her.

"Don't stop," she demanded in a husky whisper.

His low growl against her neck and the feel of his arms tightening around her was her answer. Ricki ran her left hand down over his shoulder, caressing his taut skin. It felt hot to her touch. She was shocked when a low cry of frustration escaped her when he pulled back.

"Say yes, Ricki," Ristèard demanded.

Ricki turned dazed eyes to him. "Yes to what?" She asked in a husky voice.

"Yes, to us," Ristèard said, slipping his hand up to cup her breast. "I need you tonight."

Rational thought nudged at Ricki, but she pushed it away. She was tired of always being rational, logical, calm, and in control. For one night, she wanted to be wild and free. Raising a trembling hand to touch his cheek, she pushed away the doubt. They were both adults. One night. One night, because she had no idea what would happen after it.

"Yes," she whispered, staring up into his eyes.

Chapter 15

Ristèard gently lifted Ricki into his arms and turned back toward the door leading to his bedroom. He had ordered the guard to take her to his living quarters. He had already planned to keep her there, but in the bedroom next to his before he ever kidnapped her. That was why the room had been prepared already for her arrival.

He knew he was attracted to her from the few encounters back on Kassis, but he never expected the overwhelming feelings that flooded him. He knew he was lost the moment she hit him on the head with her shoe. She had captured his heart with her defiance even as she hugged the tree in terror of heights.

Tonight, he would claim her as his Empress. His arms tightened protectively around her slender figure. He breathed in the faint scent of the shampoo that she had used to wash her hair. Turning his head, he rubbed his cheek against the soft, silky strands before pressing a kiss to her brow.

Stepping back through the door into his bedroom, he strode over to his massive bed. He carefully lowered her until her bare feet touched the thick carpet covering the polished, stone floor. Wrapping his hand around the nape of her neck, he tilted her head back and kissed her again, this time with a sense of desperation.

This was different. Before, when he fucked a woman, it was just that. He did it to relieve the pressure building inside him, but it always left him unsatisfied. This time, he was actually nervous. He wanted to take his time and explore Ricki. He wanted to bring her so much pleasure that she couldn't think of anyone other than him.

He slid the hand at her waist briefly between them and tugged loose the small bow that held the silky robe closed. Releasing his grip on her neck, he slid his hand down along her shoulder, taking the robe with him. Bursts of pleasure reverberated through him when he felt her fingers curl against his skin, her nails lightly raking his shoulders, when she felt the air against her bare shoulders.

He broke the kiss, pulling back far enough that her arms slid down his chest. He tenderly pulled on the soft material to remove it from where it had pooled around her elbows. It floated to the floor, almost as if in slow motion, landing in a semi-circle around her ankles.

Ristèard's hand trembled slightly as he raised it to touch her cheek. Drawing in a deep breath, his eyes captured every detail of her smooth complexion. The contrast between his darker skin and her fair complexion held him mesmerized.

"You are so… beautiful," he murmured in a husky voice. "I could watch you move all day. When I first saw you in the tent, I couldn't look away. The human male…," he started to ask, looking into her eyes. "What is he to you?"

Ricki's lips quirked at the corner and she raised her eyes to his. "A friend," she admitted, knowing that is all Stan could ever be now. "Stan is just a friend."

"Good," Ristèard grunted with a touch of arrogance. "Then, I will not have to kill him."

A soft, lilting chuckle escaped Ricki and she raised her hands to cup his cheeks. "No, you don't have to kill Stan," she murmured, running her thumbs back and forth against his cheek. "I see patterns dancing across your skin when I touch you. It is so beautiful."

Ristèard barely heard her softly spoken words. His eyes closed for a moment as a sharp pain of desire and something else swept through him at her tender touch. Opening his eyes, he gripped the thin straps of her gown and pulled them off her shoulders. Her gown floated down to join her robe.

"So beautiful," he muttered, lifting his hands to cup both of her breasts in them.

Ricki flushed and trembled when his thumbs ran over her taut nipples. "They are small," she murmured.

"No, they are perfect," he corrected her before leaning forward and capturing first one, then the other between his lips and sucking hard on them.

His arms swept out and caught her when her knees gave out and she started to collapse. Sweeping her up into his arms, he gently laid her on his bed. He stepped back just long enough to push the loose-fitting trousers he was wearing down.

"Ristèard," Ricki whispered. Her eyes widen in shock at his straining cock as she ran her eyes over his aroused body. "You are… beautiful."

His fists clenched at his side as he stared down at Ricki spread out on his bed. Her golden hair fanned out to one side and partially covered her right breast. Her nipples were pebbled, and a slightly darker color from his lips. His eyes moved down over her flat stomach to the soft curls between her legs. The hair was the same sun-kissed color as her long hair. Her long legs moved restlessly the longer he stared at her. In his mind, he could picture them wrapped around his shoulders as he feasted on her.

"I need you," he muttered in a guttural voice. "I… I have never felt like this before."

Ricki's eyes softened at the sudden vulnerability in his dark silver ones when he looked back at her. He knew he shouldn't admit such things to her, but something told him that she would understand. The rush of unfamiliar feelings was too much to hold inside him.

"I've never felt this way before either," she admitted, raising one slender arm up to him. "I need you, Ristèard."

The flames inside him ignited into a raging inferno. Her soft admission 'I need you' swept through him like a wildfire out of control. She needed him, not just wanted, but needed him.

Kneeling on the edge of the bed, he ran his hand along the curve of her left foot, up to her ankle. Wrapping his hand around it, he lifted it until it rested on his shoulder. A triumphant smile curved his lips when she gasped, but didn't resist. Instead, she lifted her other leg and placed it on his left shoulder. The move opened her moist core to him.

He wanted to fan the fire inside her until it was burning as hot and out of control as it was inside him. Moving slowly up between her long legs, he forced her legs farther apart. He paused briefly to press hot, nipping kisses along the inside of her thighs.

Her loud cry and passionate response echoed through the room. He breathed in her heady scent of arousal as he continued to tease her with his lips. His eyes narrowed on the moist curls protecting her hot channel. Wanting to explore, he ran his fingers down along the dark, moist slit.

He was rewarded with another smothered cry and the tightening of her heels along his back, pulling him forward. Her back bowed when he slid his finger past the curls and deep into her. The moist, heated core tightened around his finger making him groan at the answering response of his cock.

The image of him, buried to the hilt, deep inside her made his cock jerk. The brush of the tip of it against the satin sheets almost made him come. A shudder ran through his body and he had to breathe deeply to in an effort to get his body back under the thin strands of control that he was desperately trying to keep over it. Breathing deeply did not help. If anything, it ripped another thread of his control from him as the heady scent of Ricki's desire melded with his.

"Ricki," he muttered.

"I need you," she whispered in a strained voice, pressing her heels against his back and shifting restlessly. "Ristèard, I ache."

His throat closed at her words. She wasn't the only one hurting. Right now, ache was too mild of a word to use to describe the hardness of his cock and the tight pressure in his balls. He would classify it more under the terms excruciating torture.

Leaning forward, he gently spread her soft lips. His eyes lit with satisfaction when he rubbed his thumb over the small, sensitive nub. Flicking his tongue against it, he was rewarded by her loud gasp. Determined to bring her pleasure, he teased the nub while stroking her warm vaginal channel.

"Ristèard!" Ricki gasped loudly. "I... Oh my!"

Increasing the pressure, he pushed another finger deep into her. Shock coursed through him when he felt a barrier. Confusion, then comprehension, suddenly registered. A powerful wave of possessiveness shook him.

Closing his eyes, he focused on her pleasure, licking and teasing her until she exploded around him. He forced his eyes open, looking up. Her back was bowed as she shattered around him. All he could see was her flat stomach and her breasts, the nipples taut and pointed. Frustration burst through him. He wanted to see her face as she came.

Pulling back, he gently slid her legs from his shoulders so he could rise up over her. Her hands fisted the covers under her as if she was holding on to a lifeline. Her eyes were closed and her face tense as her body shuddered. Ristèard watched her eyelids flutter open when she felt his hard shaft pressing against her slick channel. Reaching down, he wrapped his fingers around first one wrist, then the other.

"Wrap your legs around my waist," he demanded, pulling her arms slightly up over her head and holding them there. "Do it, Ricki. Wrap your legs around my waist now."

He held his body frozen against hers, the tip of his cock pressed against her entrance. All it would take is one thrust to claim her as his Empress. He gritted his teeth, waiting for her to comply with his demand. He didn't want to hurt her, but he was close to losing the slim control he held over his body. A shudder ran through him when he felt her wrap her legs around his waist and press her heels into his buttocks.

"Now, you are mine," he muttered hoarsely. "My Empress."

Rocking his hips forward, he slowly pressed into her. Sweat beaded on his brow when her slick, warmth surrounded him. He could feel her body fisting his cock, stretching, as he gradually pushed into her. His breath came in small pants that matched hers when he felt the barrier once again. His head bowed until it was only a few inches from hers. Locking his eyes to her vivid pale blue ones, he slowly pushed forward through the barrier. Pain flashed through her eyes and her fingers curled into a fist, but she didn't protest.

"Ricki," he whispered in a thick voice. "I... You make me feel things inside, things that confuse me."

Releasing her wrists, he carefully lowered his body down over her, rocking his hips gently until he was buried deep inside her. Never before had he felt such a need to be gentle. The fact that he had caused her pain tore at him, even as another part of him roared in triumph at being her first lover.

Closing the distance between them, he sealed his lips over hers in a hot, possessive kiss. Strange emotions wash through him, changing, building, and crashing with each stroke. His arms tightened around her, holding her as close as he could against his body while his lips and tongue explored her mouth. He poured the emotion he was feeling into each caress.

Pulling back, he looked down at her again. He could feel his balls drawing tighter. He wanted... needed... to come, but he wanted to watch her come apart first.

"Come for me, Ricki," he demanded, his hips rocking faster, harder than before as his orgasm built. "Come for me, my Empress. Let me watch you shatter in my arms."

A shudder rocked Ricki at his words. Her hands, freed earlier from his grasp, gripped his forearms. He resisted the urge to capture her lips again when they parted, instead, focusing on her eyes as he pumped into her harder and faster. He felt her body tightening around his cock just seconds before she cried out again. Gasping, his own body exploded as she pulsed around him.

Collapsing over her body, he remembered just in time to keep his elbows locked so he wouldn't crush her. Their combined heavy breathing echoed loudly in the room. He turned his head to press a hot kiss to her temple.

"Ricki, I think I understand what it is that you make me feel," he murmured quietly in her ear.

Ricki tilted her head back enough to look at his face. "What is it that I make you feel?" She asked in a sated voice.

"Love."

Chapter 16

Ricki was stunned by Ristèard's confession. Love...
Was it possible that he could have fallen in love with
her? Doubt and confusion poured through her. If he
felt love, then what did the feelings coursing through
her mean? Was she in love with him?

Lifting her arms to hold him close, she tried to
rationalize her feelings. Yes, she had been acutely
aware of him since the first time she saw him, but she
had put that down to exasperation more than
anything else. He had been extremely arrogant... and,
well, bossy. Neither a characteristic that she found
attractive.

Still, she couldn't deny that she had agreed to go
out with Stan in an attempt to push Ristèard out of
her mind. Now, she knew that would never happen.
Pressing her lips to his shoulder, she closed her eyes
and let her hands explore his body.

There was nothing logical about the way she felt.
She wanted him physically, and the more she learned
about him, the more she acknowledged that she
enjoyed talking to him. While he was all gruff and
rough on the outside, his compassion and
determination to help his people showed a side to
him that many might not see... he was a man who
cared.

She opened her eyes when she felt him lift his
head. Another smile tugged at the corner of her lips
when she saw the scowl on his face. From the small

protrusion of his lower lip, he wasn't getting what he wanted.

"You are supposed to replied that you adore me and love me as well," he stated bluntly. "I'm waiting."

Ricki couldn't keep her chuckle of amusement from escaping. Her mind raced through her emotions, trying to name them. Did she love him? Possibly, but she wasn't ready to admit it yet. Not until she knew for sure.

"I'm deeply attracted to you," she admitted. "If I wasn't, we would not be here."

The scowl on his face deepened and his silver eyes glowed with determination. A low gasp escaped her when he shifted his hips. She could feel his cock swell inside her.

"That is not what I wanted you to say," he replied with a challenging look. "I know that you love me. I will just have to claim you again and again until you admit it. I am the only male for you now, my Empress."

Ricki's temper flared briefly at his challenge. He needed to learn that he couldn't just demand that she tell him that she loved him. She would tell him when she was good and damn ready! Her eyes widened at her thoughts.

Yes, I love him, she reluctantly acknowledged to herself.

She just wasn't ready to admit it yet. There were still too many unanswered questions and trying to deal with a relationship when she didn't even know who she was, was too much for her right now. She could handle the physical aspects. She just wasn't ready to deal with the emotional ones until she knew who she was, where she came from, and who her biological parents were.

Not to mention, saving a planet, she thought as doubts and feelings of being overwhelmed threatened to drown her.

"You are thinking too hard," Ristèard muttered, breaking into her thoughts.

"I was just thinking I needed more time to understand who and what I am and everything else that has happened," Ricki admitted, gazing up at him before a low moan escaped her when he rocked his hips. "Besides, you can't just demand that I tell you something. That isn't the way it is done. You should… Oh, that feels good," She broke off, looking up at him as intense pleasure burst through her again.

"It will feel even better before I am done," he promised in a husky voice. "Then… You will tell me you love me over and over again."

Ricki's fingers curled against the hot flesh of his back. Arching upward, she hooked her legs around the back of his thighs. The movement pushed him deeper into her.

"Maybe it will be the other way around," she teased before another low moan escaped her.

* * *

Ricki glanced back at Ristéard's sleeping form. She needed time alone to get her thoughts and emotions back under control. Last night had been…

Unexpected, foolishly impulsive, and incredible, she thought as she quietly slipped from his room and back into hers. She placed her dirty clothes on the chair before picking up some fresh ones that her mom had given her last night. She hurried into the bathroom and took a quick shower, ignoring the unfamiliar tenderness of her breasts and between her legs.

Leave it to my mom to remember the essentials when she was going on an adventure, Ricki thought in amusement as she buttoned her blouse.

Picking up the blue gown and robe, she crossed to the bed. She draped them across the end and picked up her trusty notepad. There was something soothing about being able to write something down with a pencil and paper. Technology was great, but sometimes doing things the good old-fashioned way helped her work through a problem.

Stepping quietly out of the room, she strode down the hallway and through the living room. She opened the door to the room, smiling politely at the two guards standing outside of it. Straightening her glasses, she nodded to them as she stepped out of the room.

"Ricki," Nema said, opening the door to their living quarters. "I told your dad you would be up early."

Walter came out, tucking his shirt into his pants. Ricki couldn't quite keep the smile from curving her lips. Her dad always looked neat and tidy, even in his jeans and button up shirt. His dark brown hair was slicked back and damp and he had his usual early morning scowl on his face. He was one of those people that you didn't talk to until after he had his first cup of coffee in the morning.

"Good morning, dad," Ricki murmured.

"Morning, Ricki," he grunted. "Do you think they have coffee on this planet?"

"I'm sure they do," she chuckled, turning as Marvin and Martin quietly walked up. "Hey, guys."

"Good morning, Ricki," they both replied, looking at her with an intensity that made her blush.

"Ricki, your dad and I were about to head to breakfast," Nema commented. "Do you know where we might find the kitchen?"

"I will escort you," one of the guards stated. "The Grand Ruler has asked that his Empress not be left unescorted."

Ricki's cheeks flared with color when her mom and dad looked at her with a questioning stare. Tucking a wayward strand of hair behind her ear, she glared at the guard. The color in her cheeks deepened when Marvin and Martin chuckled behind her.

"His Empress?" Walter growled. "What the hell does that mean?"

"I'll explain it later, dad," Ricki said, adjusting her glasses again out of habit. "I need to look at the door to his office and the tapestry in it again. I'll join you guys in a bit, if you don't mind. I shouldn't be long."

"I'll escort your parents to the dining room, then you back to the Grand Ruler's office," the guard said with a nod.

"That would be wonderful," Ricki replied in relief.

* * *

The small procession moved through the elegant corridors. Ricki giggled when her mom reached out and touched the walls. Brilliant threads of gold shot out against the black stone before fading. She listened absently to her parents talking about how they could use it as an attraction or part of one of the shows.

Her focus was on the beautiful paintings and the artwork on display. Different pictures hung along the corridors depicting a variety of time periods in Elpidios' history. She could spend weeks studying the ones in this corridor alone.

Releasing a sigh, she realized she was falling behind the others and hurried to catch up with them as they turned the corner. She stopped when she bumped into a woman turning the corner from the opposite direction. The impact knocked the notepad out of her hand to the floor. Before she could pick it up, the woman had knelt down.

"I'm so sorry," Ricki said in a quiet voice, glancing at the woman before looking up to see that the small group had paused in front of a sculpture farther down the corridor.

The woman was looking at the page of notes she had taken yesterday. Ricki gently took the notepad from her with an apologetic smile and closed it. For some reason, something was telling her that she should be careful about sharing her findings with anyone other than Ristéard.

"You are the female that the Grand Ruler claims as his Empress," the woman stated, looking Ricki up and down. "I am Cherissa, his consort."

Ricki's eyes widen in surprise. "That is… interesting," she replied, not really sure what else to say. "If you will excuse me, I must catch up with my parents."

Cherissa stepped in front of Ricki, blocking her way. Her eyes were narrowed as she assessed Ricki's pale complexion. Ricki took another step to the side, but the woman moved with her.

"He is finished with you for the day? If so, I will go to him. An Elpidios' male can be very aggressive when he seeks a woman to be with," Cherissa commented. "You do not look as if you could satisfy him the way I can."

Ricki's mouth tightened into a straight line. There were certain things she didn't discuss with others. Her sex life was one of those things. If Cherissa thought she was about to address that brash statement with one of her own, the woman was in for a sad surprise.

"If you will excuse me," Ricki replied in a clip tone, stepping to the left again to pass the woman. "I must catch up with my family."

Cherissa once again stepped in front of Ricki. Counting to ten slowly under her breath, Ricki swore if the woman stepped in front of her again, she was going to bitch-slap her upside her blue head. Deciding that diplomacy would not work with

Cherissa, Ricki decided being blunt about what her intentions would be if the woman didn't let her pass.

"I know how to take care of his needs," Cherissa murmured under her breath. "I know how to bring him pleasure."

Ricki glared coldly back at Cherissa. "I really don't give a damn what you know how to do. Now, I suggest you don't try to block my path again. If you do, I will remove you from it," she stated.

Cherissa looked at her with resentment. "I have a good life in the palace," she replied in a low, menacing voice. "I plan to keep it. The Grand Ruler has been pleased with my attentions until you came. I will not let you take him from me."

Ricki refused to respond to the other woman. Stepping around her, she smiled when she saw Andras glance up from where he was talking to the guard. Walking toward him, she fumbled with her notepad to hide the tears of anger in her eyes.

"Lady Ricki, is everything well?" Andras asked in concern, glancing over her shoulder at Cherissa in warning.

Ricki gave him a tight smile and nodded. "Yes," she replied, looking behind him and down the empty corridor. "My parents?"

"The guard has escorted them to break their fast," Andras replied. "He said you wished to returned to Ristéard's office for a short time."

"Yes, thank you," Ricki said with a weak smile. "There are a few things I would like to look at again."

Andras nodded, turning back so he could walk with Ricki. "You have discovered a way to save Elpidios?" He asked, glancing at her with a sharp, assessing look. "A source of Blood Stones?"

Ricki nodded. "Yes, well, maybe," she admitted reluctantly. "I'm not sure yet, but I think I'm close. I just need a little more time to see if what I've found really is what I think it is."

Andras paused as he opened a door at the end of the corridor. He looked down at her with a serious expression. His eyes flickered to the notepad in her hand before returning to her serious face.

"I truly hope you have, Empress," he replied with a sudden smile. "I really hope you have."

Me too, Ricki thought as she stepped through the doors into the corridor leading to Ristéard's office. *Me too.*

Neither one of them saw Cherissa standing at the end of the corridor watching them as they disappeared. Hatred burned in her eyes as she stared after the pale-skinned female. She hadn't been lying when she said she had it good in the palace, but that time would soon come to an end.

This world was dying and she had already been promised a nice life on another planet in exchange for information. A smile curved her lips. She couldn't remember all the information that was on the strange paper the female had, but she had recognized enough to know it was important. Tonight, she would pass it on… for a price. She wanted more than a nice life, she wanted to live like an Empress. Turning on her heel, she quickly returned to her living quarters to record what she could remember of the symbols.

* * *

Ristèard blinked several times as he came awake the next morning. Turning his head, he could see the faint light of the sun rising. For a moment, he was lost in the beauty of it. He loved his world, his people, with an intensity born from centuries of his ancestor's rule.

A deep sigh escaped him before he turned his head to look at Ricki's face. He jerked when he discovered the pillow next to his was vacant. Sitting up, he wildly looked around. The door between his room and hers was open. Throwing the covers aside, he swung his long legs over the side of it and rose.

"Ricki," he muttered under his breath.

Fear coursed through him when he strode into the other room and discovered it empty. His eyes flashed to the yellow dress, sweater, and matching shoes carefully folded on the chair while the blue nightgown was lying once again at the end of the neatly made bed.

Returning to his room, he glanced around for the loose fitting trousers he had worn the night before. They were also neatly folded, and lay on the thick, polished wood dresser. He quickly pulled them on before turning back to the door to his bedroom. Opening it, he strode through his empty living quarters to the main door leading out to the rest of the palace.

Yanking the door open, he turned his dark gaze to the two guards standing outside of his rooms. "Where is the Empress?" He demanded.

"She and her parents have returned to your office, Grand Ruler," one of the guards said.

"Were they alone?" Ristèard asked.

"No, Grand Ruler," the other guard replied. "Andras met us as I was escorting the Empress, her parents, and the two Kor d'lurs to your office. He stated he would remain with them."

Ristèard gave a sharp nod before he stepped back and shut the door. Turning on his heel, he ran his hands through his hair and released a deep, calming breath. He would have to speak with Ricki about not leaving his side. While he and Andras had killed most of the traitors yesterday, his gut was telling him that Texla and Roamlin were not the head of the serpent.

Walking back to his bedroom, he stepped into the bathroom. Pushing his trousers down, he kicked them off before stepping into the large shower. He touched the control before closing his eyes as the warm water cascaded down over his still humming body.

Ricki had been right. It had been him, not her, that had confessed his love again and again. Determination burned through him. He knew she loved him. While she had not said the words, her caressing touches had conveyed it. A reluctant smile curved his lips. His unwilling Empress was also very stubborn.

Opening his eyes, he poured a small amount of cleanser into the palm of his hands. Rubbing it into his skin, he thought of last night. They had come together over and over, each time more passionate than the last. She had explored his body with such an intensity, that just thinking about it made him hard again.

His hand fisted his wayward cock. He would have thought the damn thing would have been satisfied for at least a few hours! In his mind's eye, he remembered Ricki sliding down his body at one point. Her hand had wrapped around his cock just as he was holding it now, only she hadn't stopped with just stroking it with her hand.

A low curse escaped him when he felt his heavy sack tighten. Stroking his long length, he closed his eyes and imagined it was Ricki on her knees between his legs. Her hot, moist tongue stroking him, sucking him deep, before slowly withdrawing again.

Moaning, he braced his other hand against the wall of the shower and pumped his cock harder and faster. It didn't take long, between the image of last night and his hand, to make him spill his seed. Breathing heavily, he opened his eyes and watched as his semen mixed with the water from the shower.

Ricki should have been here with me, he thought with a touch of self-exasperation. *It would have been much more enjoyable.*

That was yet another talk, they would have to have. She needed to learn to obey him if he was to keep her safe, and keep his sanity, he reluctantly admitted. Impatient to see her now, he turned the shower off and stepped out.

Within minutes, he had dressed and was striding back out of his room toward his office. Pushing his wayward thoughts aside, he focused on what needed to be done. Ricki had discovered information that could possibly save his world. Time was running out and he needed to make a decision whether to start the evacuation of the planet and order the residents to begin moving to the underground cities.

Even if he did both, he knew tens of thousands, if not more would die. There were many of his people who would refuse to go until it was too late. He also knew that even with Elpidios' vast military and transport ships and the six large underground cities, they did not have the resources to evacuate everyone.

His eyes roamed the ancient palace that had been home to his family for centuries. Except for the brief years he and his parents had been held captive, a Roald had ruled from it. His grandfather, realizing the threat, had ordered all of its treasures be hidden in the vast catacomb systems deep inside the mountain.

For seven years, they and those that followed the Roald family, were sealed inside the only known underground city. There, they had fought to survive until they could escape and take back their rightful place. It had taken the citizens that lived above ground to finally rise up against the ruling council for them to break free.

Only when the devastation to the planet became too obvious to hide, did the citizens demand to know what was happening. Alcolsis, the cruel and greedy warlord, was no longer able to hide behind his lies. The people rose up, demanding to know what happened to his family. Massive infighting among the warlords threatened the very fabric of their existence. Alcolsis decided that he could regain control if he held the power behind the throne... The next Emperor of Elpidios, Ristèard Roald.

He would never forget the day that the traitorous councilmen came to the city with his warriors. He thought to take Ristéard as his prisoner, a young boy that he would place upon the throne and control like a master controls his pupil. Only, Ristéard already had a master that he looked up to, his father.

His father had trained with him daily, pushing him until his mind and body were prepared for the day they would seek justice. When Alcolsis had come, he and his father, along with the other men and women that had sworn loyalty to his family, struck hard and fast before the old warlord knew what had happened.

Ristéard had lost his younger brother that day, and shortly after that, his mother. But, during his time in the underground city, he had also gained others he considered his family. Andras, Emyr, Harald, and Sadao had been the same age as him when they, along with their parents and other members of their villages, were imprisoned for failing to pledge allegiance to Alcolsis.

Turning the last corner leading to his office, he paused when he saw Ricki kneeling in front of the massive doors. Two guards stood to the side, watching her with curious eyes. She was wearing a pair of dark, brown trousers and a white, long-sleeved blouse. She had her hair neatly twisted and pinned up again. At first, a sense of exasperation filled him that she insisted on confining it, that was until he saw the look of appreciation in the men's eyes.

He returned his gaze to Ricki's figure. Now that he knew what she looked like with the golden waves spread out around her, he had to admit that he was just jealous enough to want to keep it for his own private enjoyment. He also had to admit that with its length, it was easier for her to maintain.

For a moment, he just watched her with a sense of appreciation. She had the familiar clipboard in her hands that he had seen back on Kassis and was focusing back and forth between it and the door. At one point, she paused and lightly traced a pattern on the massive black panels. The way she touched it reminded him of the way she touched him last night. A low curse escaped him when he felt his body react to the memory.

He moved forward when he saw her turn her head to him. A sense of unease washed through him when instead of looking pleased to see him, her lips pressed into a hard, straight line of disapproval. His eyes followed her as she gracefully rose to her feet.

If he thought she was upset, it only took a brief glance at the smooth mask of her face and the furious look in her eyes to know that she wasn't happy to see him. Stepping closer, he nodded to the two guards who straightened and bowed their heads in acknowledgement.

"You shouldn't have left my bed," he stated bluntly, wincing when the cold fury deepened in her eyes. "I missed you," he added in a low voice meant only for her ears.

Ricki's slender shoulders shrugged. "I'm sure Cherissa would be happy to keep you warm tonight," she retorted in a clipped voice. "I believe I understand what the carvings mean. If you'd like, I can explain the information to you before I leave."

Surprise, then fury swept through Ristèard at Ricki's words. Glancing at the guards, he reached out and gripped her elbow. The guards instantly stepped forward and pulled the heavy doors open for them. He grimaced when Ricki immediately tugged her elbow out of his hand and stepped inside.

He was thankful when a swift glance confirmed that they were alone in the room. His eyes followed Ricki as she strode across the thick carpet to the window, turning only when she had placed the room and several pieces of furniture between them. Her chin lifted and she stared back at him with a glacial expression.

"Ricki," he started to say, stopping when she set the notepad in her hand down on the table next to her and raised a trembling hand to smooth a loose strand of hair back. "You have no need to be upset about Cherissa. She means nothing to me."

"That is not the impression I received this morning when she asked if you were finished with me and wanted her to come and quote 'Take care of your personal needs'. I believe that was the correct wording," she added with distaste.

Frustration and worry burned through Ristèard at the expression on Ricki's face as she repeated what Cherissa had told her. In truth, he had forgotten about not only Cherissa, but the other women he kept in the palace.

"None of them mean a thing to me, Ricki," he growled in a low voice. "The Elpidios are a very aggressive species with a high sex drive as you discovered last night. It is natural for both the male and the female of my species to release this aggression through sex."

He knew the moment he finished that he had made the situation worse, instead of better. Her eyes glistened before she rapidly blinked them. She drew in a shuddering breath and looked past him to the tapestry hanging behind his desk.

"I will go over what I believe is the key to finding the location of the hidden vault with you, before I leave this afternoon to return to Kassis with my parents," Ricki said in a voice devoid of emotion. "If you would rather, I can leave the information for you to go over later with your men and the scientists here on your world. I suggest, though, that you not delay making a decision. I talked with Ajaska this morning. He told me that Jarmen wasn't able to do much with the current shield system and confirmed what you already said, that the crystals were breaking down faster than either of you expected due to the radiation."

Ristèard took a step closer to her, clenching his fists at his side to keep from grabbing and shaking her. There was no way he would ever let her leave, especially after what happened last night. She belonged to him.

"Hear me, my Empress," he said in a low, steady voice. "You will remain by my side. Whether here on Elpidios or on a new world, you belong to me. I have claimed you as my Empress, the Empress of Elpidios. Your place is by my side now and in the future."

She returned his look with an icy gaze of her own. "I am not an object that can be claimed," Ricki replied coolly, picking up her notepad. "Now, if you have finished wasting my time, I have more important matters that require my attention. I promised my parents that I would join them for breakfast once I was finished."

"Ricki," Ristèard murmured, unable to keep the distance between them any longer. "Ricki, look at me... Please."

It took several long seconds before she turned her face back to his. The glistening in her eyes was back, only this time, one fragile, liquid diamond had escaped to slide down from the corner of her eye. Raising his hand, he caught the tear on the tip of his finger. The light shining through the window caught on it, and for a moment, he could see his reflection in it. Lifting it to his lip, he captured the salty moisture on his tongue.

"I won't be like that woman or the other ones you... you... have here," Ricki whispered, turning her face away again so he couldn't see the hurt in her eyes. "It was only for one night. It is best for me to go back to Kassis where I belong."

Ristèard hated the way she stiffened and tried to withdraw from his touch. Sliding his hands up to cup her cheeks between them, he gently rubbed her soft skin with his thumbs. She had lowered her eyelids to prevent him from seeing her eyes. He patiently waited for her to look up at him. When she didn't, he leaned down and touched his lips tenderly to hers.

"They mean nothing to me, Ricki Bailey," he murmured huskily against her lips. "It is you that has captured my heart. I need you. I have never told another that, not my friends, not my father, and never another woman. I need you, Ricki, like I need the air to breathe. For me, there is only you, my Empress."

He felt the shuddering breath that she slowly inhaled. It took several long seconds before her eyelids lifted and she stared up at him with wounded, untrusting eyes. Once again, he felt like he was falling into the clear, blue lakes found high in the mountains of his world.

"How can I believe you?" She asked. "You say you love me, but you don't know me. How can you, when I don't even know who I am? How do I know that you won't use me like you do those other women? How... How do I know that you would be happy with just me?"

Ristèard released a low moan and captured her lips in a heated kiss filled with the churning emotions deep inside him. He poured every ounce of love and need into it. His arms slid down around her body to pull her up against him. When he finally released her lips, they were both breathing heavily.

"Feel my heart," he said gruffly. "Feel it and know that it thunders for you, Ricki. You say that I do not know you, but I do. The first time I saw you, was in the huge tent back on Kassis. I saw a woman that cared about those around her. I saw a woman who respected the knowledge and skills of her people. The night of the performance, when you knew that the ones you loved would be in danger, you remained calm in the face of it. I watched you, Ricki, and knew that you were mine, even before I understood why. The prophecy told of your coming, yet I had no desire or belief that I would need a bride until I met you. Last night, I saw you in a way no man has ever seen you before and I fell more in love with you."

Ricki released a delicate snort and a blush rose up her cheeks. She looked at him as if he had lost his mind. Maybe he had, but if he had to lose it, he couldn't think of a better way. Bending forward, he pressed another tender kiss to her lips before pulling back reluctantly when the door behind him opened.

"What is it, Andras?" He asked in a low, hard voice, not turning away from Ricki.

"I'm sorry to interrupt, Ristèard, I was just checking on Lady Ricki to make sure she was safe and to see if she was ready to join her parents," Andras quietly replied.

Ristèard glanced over his shoulder. "I will escort her," he responded. "I need for you to prepare for my departure. We will need a transport and several days rations."

"Do you wish for me to recall Harald and Emyr to travel with us?" Andras asked with a raised eyebrow. "They are still overseeing the zones."

Ristèard shook his head. "No, Sadao will travel with Ricki and I as we make our way to the hidden Temple of the Empress," he decided. "I want you to remain here to monitor the shields and make sure there are no more attacks."

"As you wish," Andras said, bowing his head in acknowledgement.

"Andras," Ristèard called when Andras started to turn. "While I am gone, I want you to review the video and data on Texla and the other council members that attacked us. Also, speak with Manderlin and see if he can shed any light on who is behind this. My gut is telling me that whoever has been behind the attacks, will strike again, especially now that there might be a way to save the planet."

Andras paused, his eyes briefly flickered to Ricki before they returned to Ristèard. "I will let you know as soon as I find anything."

"One last thing," Ristéard said, staring intently into Andras' eyes. "See that Cherissa is removed from the palace."

A cold smile curved Andras' lips. "I will see to that personally," he replied, withdrawing from the room.

Chapter 17

"Suck it up, Blueboy, we're going," Walter stated, nodding to Marvin and Martin. "Make sure you have Nema's things, will you boys?"

Marvin grinned at his brother. "No problem, Walter. Nema has already asked us," he replied in a slightly accented voice. "She has your's and Ricki's bags packed as well."

"I need to remember to thank mom for bringing me some clothes," Ricki replied, checking the satchel with her notepads and tablets. "Dad, are you sure you and mom should go? It could be dangerous. We don't know what we are going to find there."

Ristèard scowled as he listened to the chaos in the room. It didn't help when he heard Ajaska's soft chuckle behind him. The Kassisan was enjoying his frustration far too much.

"You know that your laughing about this is not building a good diplomatic relationship, don't you?" Ristèard grumbled under his breath. "How do you deal with that human? He has no concept of what I could do to him."

Ajaska looked in amusement at him. "I have watched him with the others. He has a very commanding presence, can be very gruff, but he has a good heart," he observed.

Ristéard rubbed the back of his neck and watched as Martin picked up the items Walter was referring to and placed them on the back of the air skids that he and Marvin would be using. He had escorted Ricki to break their fast while Andras organized the equipment they would need for their journey. What he had not expected was her parents insistence that they accompany them. Of course, Marvin and Martin refused to allow them to go without their protection, which led to Ajaska shrugging his shoulders and informing him that he was also going along.

"I might as well accompany you. You could use someone to cover your back and my new daughters would kill me if anything happened to Walter, Nema, or Ricki. Besides, I am curious about Lady Ricki's findings," Ajaska had commented. "Jarmen has also requested more time to analyze why your shields keep failing. He is fascinated by their structure and the technology behind it."

Ristéard knew exactly why the shields kept failing. Someone was sabotaging them. The failures had started shortly after his first meeting with Ajaska. At first, he had suspected it might have been a covert attack by the Kassisans to test their technology and responses. He had quickly dismissed that notion after he visited their world.

"Do you have any idea of who is behind the attacks on you?" Ajaska asked quietly, pulling Ristéard back to the present situation.

Ristéard shook his head. "I have Andras going through every record, every person involved from the lowest level to the highest. It has only been since I met with you that the attacks have escalated to the shield stations," he said warily.

Ajaska gave him a sharp glance. "You are not suggesting that I or any of my people are to blame, are you?" He asked with an edge to his voice. "It is better to have my people as your ally than your enemy."

"No, I do not think you or the Royal House is behind the attacks," Ristéard replied thoughtfully, watching Ricki as she knelt in front of her mom who had just joined them. He could see the concern on her face as well as the resignation. She was just as frustrated with her parents' determination to come with them as he was. "What confuses me is the attacks have been random and easily fixed until the past few days."

Ajaska turned his head to study where Ristéard was looking. A frown creased his brow. His eyes darkened with concern.

"You think it is because of Ricki, don't you?" Ajaska observed. "The attacks have increased since you learned about her."

"Yes," Ristéard murmured. "That is why I don't want her out of my sight. I fear that whoever is behind the attacks on the shields will target her next."

Ajaska's lips curved up at the corner. "You are in love with her," he stated with a satisfied nod. "I must admit, I find human women fascinating."

Ristéard looked at Ajaska in surprise, but didn't say anything. Yes, they were fascinating. It was more than their unique coloring, it was the way they approached things. While the Kassisan females were sheltered and considered fragile, the Elpidios women were forced by the history of their world to be more aggressive, much like the males. The human women contained a balance between the two; Fragile, yet strong at the same time. The strength was more internal, than physical, or at least it appeared that way until he remembered the amazing feats Ricki's friends, River, Star, and Jo had completed during the fight with Tai Tek.

A reluctant smile curved his lips as he watched Ricki lean forward and brush a kiss across her mother's cheek. *Ricki's friends were not the only strong ones,* he thought with a wry grin. *She did a pretty good job of knocking me on my ass more than once.*

"It is time to leave," he suddenly said. "We should reach the area just before dark. I do not want to take an airship. There are still tribal groups there that hold that area as being sacred lands. The air skids can come in under their surveillance, but we will still need to travel with care."

"I've been wanting to get my hands on one of your bikes since the first time I saw one," Ajaska replied, rubbing his hands together. "How fast can they go?"

Ristéard grinned. "They are my personal design," he said, turning to walk over to the solid black air bike. "Fast enough when the need arises."

Ristéard's eyes connected with Ricki's worried ones. He held out his hand to her. She would ride behind him, while her father rode with Martin, and her mother with Marvin. Sadao and Ajaska would take the rear and carry most of the supplies on their air bikes.

Each of them were dressed in an environmentally controlled black body suit designed for the brutal heat of the Eastern desert day and the extreme cold of the night. It had been a challenge getting one modified for Walter and Nema at such short notice and was another reason why they were running more than three hours past the time he had wanted to leave. As it was, he wasn't positive they would make it to the edge of the mountains before dark.

"Thank you," Ricki murmured in a low voice, taking the black helmet he held out.

"For what?" Ristéard asked in surprise.

Ricki glanced to the side where Marvin was lifting her mom onto the back of the air skid and making sure she was not only comfortable, but also secure. A sigh escaped her as she returned her attention back to Ristéard. Her emotions were all over the place right now. She was still hurt by her earlier encounter in the hallway with Cherissa and not sure what to believe or not believe.

"For being patient and for allowing my parents to go, even if I would prefer they returned to the warship," she admitted.

Ristéard cupped her cheek and leaned close enough to brush a kiss across her lips. "It is a father's right to protect his daughter," he replied before giving her a wry grin. "Besides, he threatened to kick my ass if I tried to stop him."

A chuckle escaped Ricki and a soft, rosy flush colored her cheeks when she looked back at her dad and realized that everyone was waiting on them. Lifting the helmet, she slid it over her head. Immediately, the solid black shield lit with a soft green glow and she could see the inside of the underground cavern that housed Ristéard's private transports. On the left side of the front shield was a series of information telling her the temperature outside, her location, and her communication link with Ristéard.

"Can you hear me?" His deep voice echoed in her ears.

Ricki nodded before grimacing. "Yes, sorry," she answered in a husky voice.

"If you need to connect with any of the others in the group, just say their names," Ristéard explained. "I have linked my helmet with yours, so I can monitor your systems. If you feel uncomfortable or need anything, let me know."

"I'll be fine," she replied, sliding on the back of the air skid and gripping the handgrips that rose up. "Let's go save your planet."

"Our planet," Ristéard corrected, huskily. "This is your world now as well, my Empress."

Ricki didn't respond. She didn't want to admit the overwhelming fear coursing through her that she might be wrong. What if she had misinterpreted the information? What if it had just been an elaborate story carved into the door to give people hope when there was no hope? What if…

No, she thought fiercely, pushing her fear and doubts away.

There was a way to save Elpidios. The thought that so many people could die threatened to choke her. The loud roar from the crowd when Ristéard had lifted their joined hands still left a sense of stunned disbelief inside her.

For a moment, she remembered the look on the faces of the children as they stood there. She had walked down the platform, unable to ignore their outstretched arms. Brushing the guards concern away, she had touched their small hands, giving them a squeeze and murmuring to them. It was when she had risen and looked into the pleading eyes of their parents, that she realized that she couldn't turn and walk away. They knew that their planet was dying, yet she also saw hope and renewed determination.

Ricki curled her fingers tightly around the bar in front of her as the air skid lifted. Swallowing, she could feel the sense of panic build as it rose from the ground. She glanced to the side, breathing a sigh of relief when she realized that it was only about four feet to the ground. She could step down if she needed too. Four feet wasn't bad, she could handle that.

"Breathe, Ricki," Ristéard murmured in her ear.

Ricki looked back up, staring at the back of his helmet. "I'm breathing," she muttered. "I was afraid it might go higher, but this isn't so bad."

She should have known from the husky chuckle in her ear that she was in trouble. She didn't know why she hadn't put two and two together. Of course they were only a few feet off the ground, they were inside a tunnel system under the palace. That changed the moment they broke out of the restrictive walls. That was when she released more of the words she didn't realize she knew in Ristéard's ear. The first ones starting with 'Oh, shit!'

Chapter 18

Ricki pierced Ristéard with another annoyed look when he grinned at her. Turning her back on him, she tugged on the black knit cap that her mother had pulled out of the never-ending supply of items she had packed. She had to admit she was thankful her mother was so resourceful. Not so much for her, but for them as she thought of how chilly it was compared to earlier. The suits might regulate their bodies, but they would need a cover for their heads with the stiff wind that was blowing.

"Are you cold?" Ristéard asked, coming up behind her.

Ricki glanced over her shoulder and scowled at him. "No," she said, before reluctantly admitting why. "I've never had a problem with the cold, it is the heat that bothers me. Mom was always on me when I was little to wear my sweater, or put on warmer clothes, but I loved it when the weather cooled off, and when we traveled to countries where it was frequently cold. Now, I think I understand why."

Ristéard watched as Ricki raised her left hand and concentrated for a few seconds. Delicate ice crystals formed on the tips of her fingers. He jerked back when she suddenly twisted her hand and pointed it away from where they were standing. A burst of ice shot from the center of her palm.

His arm slipped around her when she swayed and her knees buckled. Concern darkened his gaze as he stared down into her pale face. Her eyes were closed and she was breathing shallow.

"Ricki?"

Her eyelashes fluttered before her eyelids slowly lifted. "Sorry," she whispered. "I wasn't expecting that. It, sort of, drained me."

Ristéard snorted, lifting her in his arms and carried her to their shelter that he had set up just a short time before. They had made good time considering they had covered over twenty-four hundred kilometers of treacherous terrain. The last hour had been done in almost complete darkness.

They had settled the air skids at the foot of the mountains, closest to the position Ricki had determined would take them to the entrance to the maze. He had ordered Martin and Marvin to take the first watch, knowing the two Kor d'lurs were excellent at mapping and blending into their environments. Sadao had set up a perimeter defense system while Ajaska helped Walter and Nema set up their shelter for the night.

He had set up his and Ricki's shelter before moving away from the group to contact Andras. They talked for several minutes before he shut down communications and returned to camp. Concern washed through him when he saw Ricki standing off to the side in the darkness.

She had said some very interesting words at the beginning of their journey. It had taken him almost an hour of talking to her in a quiet, soothing tone before she finally calmed down enough to breathe normally.

He had suggested taking her back to the palace when her pulse spiked alarmingly. She had refused, but he knew she had a death grip on the air skid. Ristéard's pride and admiration for her continued to grow as she fought to overcome her fear of heights as they sped toward the Eastern Mountains.

He shouldered his way through the thin fabric barrier of the shelter. His arms tightened around her when she moved restlessly. Bending, he gently laid her down on the soft bedding.

"Do not move," he ordered, reaching into the small pack next to the bed. Pulling a scanner out, he slowly ran it over her. "You are dehydrated."

Returning the scanner to the bag, he pulled out a small flask and held it to her lips. He waited until she drank almost half of it before he pulled it away from her lips. Cupping her cheek, he ran his gaze over her face.

"I'm fine," she whispered. "It just took me by surprise. I wasn't expecting that, the ice just… came out."

"Well, don't let it happen again," he growled. "I don't like what it does to you. Have you eaten?"

Ricki shook her head and grimaced. "I forgot," she admitted. "I tend to do that when I get focused on something."

Ristéard sat back on his heels and rummaged through the bag again. This time, he pulled out a small package. He pressed a button on the corner. A red light lit up for several seconds, before it flashed green. He ripped the cover off of it and a fragrant aroma filled the shelter.

He slid a thin spork-looking utensil out of the lid and placed it in the food tray. Sitting forward again, he used one arm to help her sit up. He shook his head when she started to reach for the tray.

"Let me," he said, lifting the spork to her mouth.

Ricki rolled her eyes. "I can feed myself," she complained. "I…."

Ristéard took the opportunity to slip more food between her protesting lips. It was the first time he had ever cared for someone else. His brow furrowed in concentration as he continued to feed her.

"I've never done this before," he said quietly. "I remember my mother feeding my younger brother. I would watch her as she cared for him. He was born early and was very sick. The only medicine we had were the few herbs my mother and a few other women grew."

Ricki swallowed the warm liquid he was feeding her. Her mind flashed to the painting on the wall above the fireplace in his office. She remembered in the background a woman holding the body of a small child and the grief in the older man's eyes.

"The painting," she murmured. "That was you and your father in the center. Was the woman holding the child behind you, your mother and brother?"

Ristéard nodded, looking down at the empty container of food. "I don't think of them often anymore. There has been so much death since then and there will be more, much, much more, if I cannot find a way to save my world," he admitted.

"How old... How old were you when you were sent down to the prison?" Ricki asked hesitantly, drawing her legs up and wrapping her arms around her knees.

Ristéard set the empty tray next to the bag and nudged her over to the other side of their makeshift bed. Once she had scooted over, he pulled the thermal sheet over them and lay back, taking her with him as he lay down. For several minutes, they laid in silence. The only sounds were the soft voices of her parents and Ajaska talking and the wind as it swept through the mountains above them. Somewhere out there were the two brothers. He and Sadao would take the second watch in a few hours.

"I was ten when my grandfather was murdered," he said, wrapping his arm around her and pulling her closer. "They attacked late at night. I understand now that it was a culmination of centuries of disagreements and power struggles between the various warlords that led up to it." He paused for a moment giving Ricki time when she rolled onto her side so she could rest her head on his shoulder. Her hand lay gently over his heart. A deep sigh escaped him and he relaxed before continuing his story.

"My great, great grandfather had been increasingly vocal about the amount of Blood Crystals the warlords were mining and selling off-world. He was the one who had pushed for the warlords to form a council in an effort to stabilize the harvesting and

190 ~ S.E. Smith

sale of the Blood Crystals. He wanted each zone to realize just how much of what they were doing was affecting not just their areas, but the entire world. It took almost a century for the scientists to admit that the gradual increase in radiation was caused by the dwindling amount of Blood Crystals. They suggested setting up the shields in an effort to slow the process until more Blood Crystals could either be found or replicated. A small reserve of the crystals were stored to power the shields and provide a source for replication. Then, during my grandfather's time, a young and powerful warlord named Alcolsis was elected to represent his zone. He was a cruel and greedy man. He convinced the other warlords on the council that my grandfather was making up the information so that he could control the Blood Stones, and thus control Elpidios."

A shiver went through Ricki. She had heard or read the same type of stories over and over throughout history. It would appear that it didn't matter which world or species it was, greed and power played a significant role. She didn't know why it surprised her as much as it did. Throughout the animal kingdom, it was the way of life.

"What happened?" She asked.

His arms tightened around her, one caressing her hip, while the other one ran a tender path up and down the arm lying on his chest. Something told her that he had never shared what happened with another. Only those that had been there really knew.

"My mother was pregnant with my brother," he murmured. "She came into my room and woke me. I could hear the sounds of fighting. My father and grandfather, along with the security force loyal to them, fought against Alcolsis' forces, but there were too many. He had combined the forces of the other warlords and taken control. A dozen of Alcolsis' men broke through the door to my bedroom. One of them struck my mother when she tried to stop them, knocking her out. I tried to protect her, but there were too many of them and I was too young."

"It must have been terrifying," Ricki whispered. "No child should go through something like that."

"No," he agreed. "But, for me, I think it is worse for a child to grow up knowing that their planet is dying."

Another shiver ran through Ricki's body as she thought of Earth. How would she feel if she knew it was dying? Even worse, how would she feel if she brought a child into the world knowing that they would almost surely die or would be forced to leave their home for someplace unknown.

"Oh, Ristéard," she choked, turning her face into his neck. "It must be heartbreaking."

For several minutes, he didn't say anything. What could he say? Yes, it is heartbreaking to watch the home you love die? That the feelings of helplessness sometimes almost drown him in their intensity? It was only his determination to not let it happen that kept him going some days. Before Ricki, he had nothing but his drive to save his world to keep him going.

"Alcolsis executed my grandfather before us," he continued in an emotionless voice. "The next day, we were transported to the underground city of Elipsis. There, anyone who did not swear allegiance to Alcolsis was imprisoned." A bitter smile curled his lip. "What Alcolsis didn't expect was the advancement of the people that lived there before us or our will to survive. Our people had lived for centuries below ground before, using the natural elements contained underneath the surface of Elpidios to build and prosper. Every few months, a shipment of supplies was delivered. My father suspected it was by the families of those held captive."

"Did you have any family above ground still?" She asked.

Ristéard shook his head, his hand pausing on her arm. "No," he replied in a quiet voice. "The only family left was my father, my mother, and my little brother who was born in the underground city a few weeks after we were sealed in. He was almost two months early and the healer imprisoned with us didn't think he would live through the night. He did, but he was very sick, as were many of the other young children. The scientists studying the period and the underground city later learned there was a type of fungus growing in the caverns that released spores into the air. Our immune system would normally not be affected by it, but those that were very young, sick, or elderly could not fight against it. It would settle in their lungs and they would slowly drown. My brother, Erindos, was seven when he died. My mother never fully regained her strength after his birth and passed away just days after we were freed. My father devoted his life to righting the wrong done to our world. I have continued his fight."

"I'm so sorry, Ristéard," Ricki whispered. "You've been through so much. To live through that, and to have the fate of your world on your shoulders, must be overwhelming at times."

He released a low chuckle. "I have very broad shoulders," he teased, before sobering. "Sleep now, my beautiful Empress. Tomorrow, I plan to give hope back to my world."

Ricki snuggled closer, enjoying the feel of his arms. A reluctant smile curved her lips as she remembered him telling her about some of the mischief he, Andras, and the other men with him used to get into, in an effort to distract and calm her when he had increased their altitude during the flight. For as gruff and arrogant as his persona was, he really was a man who cared deeply under all the rough edges. The stress from the day, combined with a lack of sleep the night before, lured her into an exhausted sleep.

I'm definitely falling in love with him, she thought as she faded into the vivid world of a young boy and his adventures in a magical underground city.

A satisfied grin curved Ristéard's lips at Ricki's softly whispered words. He knew she didn't realize she had spoken aloud, but he had heard her. One step at a time, he reminded himself. To reach the top of the mountain, he needed to focus on the step ahead of him. It would be the same with Ricki.

Chapter 19

Ristéard glanced down at the scanner in his hand. He turned as Sadao moved down the rocky surface toward him. The grim look on Sadao's face told him that the scanners weren't wrong, they were about to have company.

He glanced up at the sky. Already, the horizon to the east showed the early morning light on it. His lips tightened into a line of frustration as he counted the number of heat images on the screen.

"Twenty-five," Sadao confirmed, sliding on the slippery surface and kneeling on one knee beside him. "I can lead them away while you get the others to safety."

Ristéard shook his head. "They have spread out, I counted another ten images coming up from different angles." Touching the comlink attached to his ear, he waited for Ajaska to answer. "Wake Walter, Nema, and Ricki. We have company."

"They are already awake," Ajaska replied in a calm voice. "How many?"

"Thirty-five, maybe more," Ristéard replied in a clipped tone. "Tell Marvin and Martin that Ricki is to be protected at all cost. I want them to get her away from here now."

"What of Walter and Nema?" Ajaska asked in concern.

Ristéard closed his eyes as he thought of the small couple. Ricki would not like the decision he was making, but she was the key to his world's survival. As a leader, he sometimes had to make the decisions that he didn't like, especially when he knew the outcome could result in death.

"Ricki is the priority," he replied harshly. "My world needs her. She is the only one that matters."

Silence greeted his statement before he heard Ajaska's hard voice. "I'll order them to take her."

"Sadao and I are returning to camp," Ristéard said, severing the connection. He glanced at Sadao and nodded. "Let's go."

"How will the Kor d'lur get her past those surrounding us?" Sadao asked under his breath.

Ristéard glanced at Sadao's concerned face. "They can blend in with the surroundings. If they cover Ricki, we could walk right by and never see them," he said.

Sadao looked surprised. "How do you know this?" He asked curiously. "I have never seen one of them before."

Ristéard didn't have a chance to respond. Instead, he jerked to a stop and held up his hands when he suddenly found that they were surrounded. The figures, covered from head to toe in the same colors of the sand and rocks, carried long power rods in their hands. The tips of the rods glowed the same red as the Blood Stones.

Rage and frustration welled up from deep inside him as he thought about how close, and yet how far, he was from the goal he had spent his life working toward. He kept his eyes on the smaller figure in front of him. Manderlin had warned him about a tribal group that lived along the base of the Eastern Mountains.

"They are like ghosts, moving in and out among the mountains," Manderlin had quietly told him when he visited him shortly before they left. He had wanted to check on the elderly councilman and to thank him for standing and fighting beside him when Texla had attacked. "There is little reason to travel to that area as it is barren for the most part. There are the sands of the desert to the east and the rugged rocks of the mountains to the west. Few individuals live there and it is said to be haunted with the spirits of the creatures that once attacked our world."

"How can they survive if the land is so harsh?" Ristéard asked. "Surely they must exchange with some of the merchant travellers?"

Manderlin had tiredly shaken his head, wincing when he jarred his still healing wound. "Nay, the few that have survived an encounter with them speak of hideous, black-eyed creatures that carry deadly sticks that glow with the blood of the dead."

Ristéard had a better appreciation for what Manderlin meant. The creatures wore large, rounded covers over their eyes. The covers were black, and more than likely helped to prevent sand and the sun from blinding them. Their clothing helped camouflage them. What captured his attention was the glow of the Blood Stone on the tips of their staffs. He had not seen crystals that large since he was a very young boy.

"I demand you let us pass," he said harshly, glaring at the three figures standing silently in front of him.

His eyes flashed when they suddenly parted and another figure, this one larger than the others, stepped forward. The cloaked figure studied him for several long seconds before he flicked his hand. Ristéard heard Sadao's shout of warning when the three smaller creatures lowered the staffs and pointed it at them just as a burst slammed into his chest.

He fought against the darkness threatening to take him for a fraction of a second after he collapsed. His eyes blinked rapidly as his vision blurred and the shadowy figures surrounded him. He didn't feel his body being lifted and carried across the uneven ground or see the way the large creature paused to look as the bodies of the others in his party were also taken.

* * *

Ricki peered between the stiff bodies of Marvin and Martin. Shock had coursed through her when Ajaska bit out a harsh order for the two men to hide her. She had fought when she realized that they were leaving her parents behind.

"No!" Ricki cried out, turning toward her mom and dad. "Take them, I'll follow."

Marvin had grabbed her and pulled her back against his body, looking worriedly at his brother. "We can fight," he told Ajaska. "Few things can harm us in our shifted state."

"We can't take the chance, Marvin," Ajaska stated. "Ristéard is right. Ricki is the priority. She must be protected at all cost."

"Mom," Ricki whispered, tears streaming down her cheeks.

"You go with Marvin and Martin, Ricki," her dad ordered. "I'll protect your mother. Ristéard knows that you are the key to saving his world. He is doing what needs to be done."

"No!" Ricki hissed in dismay, looking at her dad and shaking her head. "I won't leave you two."

Nema pulled away from Walter and hurried over to Ricki. "You do as your father says, Ricki," Nema said sternly. "We'll be fine, and if not... Well, we'll be together."

"You have to think of what is at stake, Ricki. It is more than you or your parents, it is an entire planet," Ajaska interjected. "There is no time to argue."

The weight of responsibility struck her hard. Her mother had squeezed her hand before returning to her dad's opened arms. Nodding, she shrank back against Marvin. She felt him shift as the hard plates covered his body. This time, they were the same color as the rocks around them. A moment later, Martin's hard body had closed around her until she was cocooned between them with only a very narrow line of vision.

She bit down on her fist when she saw the first shadowy figures slip into her line of view. Her dad roared out in rage. She heard her mother's cry of fear before everything went silent. Tears blinded her a moment later when she saw the limp bodies of her parents being held in the arms of several of the creatures. Another was talking, but she couldn't hear what he was saying. She pushed against Martin's stiff body, but it was like pushing against the stones littering the area around their camp.

Bowing her head, she silently cried. If Ajaska and her parents had been taken, she had no doubt that so had Ristéard and Sadao. Closing her eyes, she waited until Marvin and Martin felt it was once again safe.

* * *

Ricki rose stiffly, nodding to Martin when he slid a hand under her elbow to help her up. She looked around with worried eyes. The creatures had taken everything, including the air skids. She shivered. She knew shock was setting in. Tugging the black cap lower, she wrapped her arms around her waist and turned to face the mountain.

"What do we do now?" She whispered, staring up at the jagged points.

Marvin came up and stood next to her. "We find what we came for," he replied, laying a soothing hand on her shoulder.

Tears burned her eyes again, but she blinked them back. "And what about my parents and the others? What about... Ristéard? Shouldn't we go after them, try to help them?" She asked, turning to look up at him. "You swore to protect my parents."

Marvin's face softened and he looked to his brother for guidance. A moment later, Martin stood in front of her. He raised his hand and brushed the back of it across her cheek.

"You have always been our first priority," Martin replied, glancing back toward the mountain. "Something tells me that if we find the maze, we will find the others as well."

"I agree," Marvin said quietly. "I think those that were here guard the treasure that we seek, Ricki."

Ricki's jaw tightened and her face drew into the cool, calm mask that she wore when she didn't want others to know what she was feeling. Turning back to both men, she raised her chin in determination.

"Then let's go find the treasure," she said calmly.

Marvin's lips curved upward in approval. "It might be dangerous," he warned her.

Ricki's eyebrow rose and she raised her hand. Ice swirled from the tips, forming a long, sharp blade. She gazed at it for a moment before she looked back at the two men standing before her.

"So, am I," she replied coolly. "Let's go."

Chapter 20

Ristéard looked up at the tall entrance carved into the side of the mountain. The figure of the First Empress of Elpidios was carved above the doorway where she looked down on those that entered the mountain. A series of pillars rose up to support the roof of the entrance. He swallowed when he saw that the dozen huge supports were carved from Blood Stone. That much crystal would power the shields for a couple of years. A dozen steps led up to the twenty-foot tall entrance. Beyond it, was inky darkness.

He staggered forward when the creature behind him pushed him in the back with the long staff he carried. His gaze swung to Sadao and Ajaska when they stumbled to a stop next to him. The three of them now stood side by side. Glancing briefly over his shoulder, he heard Walter angrily snap at one of the figures standing near him.

"You touch my wife and I'll shove that staff up your ass," he growled, pulling Nema closer to him. "Just point where you want us to go, damn it. We don't need you shoving us or pointing those damn things at us to do it."

Ajaska's low chuckle echoed through the group. "I always did love a good fight," he said. "What about you, Ristéard?"

Ristéard shook his head. The Kassisan warrior had a strange sense of humor that he was still trying to understand. How he could think being tied up was a laughing matter, he would never know. Ristéard reluctantly stepped forward when the tall figure he remembered from before turned and silently looked down at him.

Silently following the figure, he blinked as his vision adjusted to the darker interior. It didn't take long for him to realize that they were crossing a long narrow footbridge. Sadao's loud hiss of shock confirmed what he had already noticed, the entire bridge was made of the crystals as well.

"How did all our explorations and searches miss this?" Sadao whispered in awe. "This many Blood Stones could save our world for several more years."

Ristéard had already thought the same thing, but he didn't want to just save it for a few more years, he wanted to save it for hundreds of centuries to come. He didn't want future generations of Elpidios children to be born wondering if they would one day have to leave their world or die. He wanted them to live, grow, and plan for a future.

I want a future, he silently admitted. *I want a future for my sons and daughters.*

His thoughts turned to Ricki. He wished he'd had one more chance to see her, to be with her. Regret filled him at only having the one night with Ricki. He wanted hundreds, thousands, more.

"Ristéard, look!" Ajaska's voice echoed as they neared the end of the bridge and saw the bright glow of the large room on the other side. "I think you have found your treasure!"

Ristéard stared at the brilliant reflection of the chamber. The polished walls glowed a dark red. Everything in the room was made from the Blood Stones; the walls, the floors, the chairs and alter, even the ceiling. The small group stopped in the center of the room. Ristéard rotated in a slow circle taking in the entire area.

"Will you look at that?" Nema whispered, staring up at the ceiling. "I've never seen anything so beautiful before."

Ristéard glanced up. From the ceiling, large deposits of crystals hung in majestic spirals. His eyes moved back to the tall figure that paused before a tapestry similar to the ones that hung in his office. In the center of the tapestry was an image that looked eerily like Ricki when she stood looking down at him from the tree by the river on Kassis.

A sharp pain lanced through him as he stared at it. Her hair was unbound like it had been that night and was blowing around her in wild abandon. There was a look of determination in her eyes and her chin jutted forward just like Ricki's did when she was feeling stubborn. He drank in her beauty, knowing he would never get tired of looking at her.

In his mind's eye, he could see her spread on his bed looking up at him with her vivid blue eyes. Keeping his gaze on it, he stepped forward.

"You look as if you have seen the Empress before," a husky voice stated.

Ristéard reluctantly pulled his gaze away from the tapestry. He swallowed and gave a sharp nod. The figure reached up and slowly pulled the mask shielding its face off. Surprise lit his eyes when he saw it was a female. She was a slightly lighter blue than most Elpidios' females.

"Where?" The female asked. "Where do you know the female?"

"She's my daughter," Nema said in a soft voice, staring up at the tapestry as well. "That's our Ricki."

The female stared down at Nema and Walter in confusion. They looked nothing like the Empress with their dark coloring. Then, again, they didn't look like any species she had ever seen before.

"Who is this Ricki?" The female asked, tilting her head. "Where is she?"

"Where is the vault?" Ristéard interjected in a harsh voice, flashing a look of warning at Nema and Walter. "What is in it?"

The female turned and looked back at Ristéard. Her face was hard and her shoulders stiffened. Twirling the staff in her hands, she struck him across the jaw with the blunt end of it. He stumbled backwards, but didn't fall.

"How do you know of the sacred vault?" The woman demanded. "How did you discover this location?"

Ristéard spit out the blood where he had bitten the inside of his cheek when she struck him. He slowly turned his head glare at her. His own eyes promised that he wouldn't forget her attack.

"Because I told him," a soft voice said, pushing through the crowd of cloaked figures.

* * *

Ricki stared down at the line of cloaked figures. They were moving into a line to pass through an especially narrow cut in the rocks. Marvin and Martin were moving in on the last figure in the long line.

It hadn't taken long to catch up with group. How the two brothers were able to track the group on the rocky surface, she would never know. She was just thankful to have their expertise. They had warned her to stay hidden in the cluster of rocks until they returned.

She winced when she saw Marvin grab the figure from behind and drag them out of sight. She bit her lip and crawled back until she was standing once again in the shadowed alcove of the rocks. It didn't take long for them to return, the unconscious figure tossed over Marvin's shoulder.

He stepped forward and lowered the body to the ground. Martin quickly pulled the mask covering the creature's face off. All three of them sat back, stunned when the face of a young woman was revealed.

"You didn't kill her, did you?" Ricki asked fearfully. "She is young, little more than a child."

"No," Marvin replied. "I was going to until I realized how small the creature was," he admitted reluctantly.

"Get the cloak off," Martin instructed. "We don't have much time. Ricki, you will wear it and fall into line behind the others. Marvin and I will follow behind the group."

"Just remember," Marvin said. "If it becomes too dangerous or you are discovered, our first priority is to get you out."

Ricki nodded. "What about her?" She asked in concern. "We can't just leave her here."

Martin touched Ricki's chin, tilting it toward him. His eyes were sad, but determined. She knew immediately that she wasn't going to like what he had to say.

"We will secure her in such a way that she will eventually be able to free herself, but we cannot take her with us," Martin replied. "This is not a time to let your heart guide you, Ricki. You must do what is necessary to get inside the mountain."

Ricki glanced back down at the peaceful face of the young girl. Yes, she knew she shouldn't let her heart guide her, but she also had to be true to who she was. Drawing in a deep breath, she nodded.

"As long as she will be able to free herself," she insisted, taking the cloak that Marvin held out to her and rising so she could slip it on over her clothing. She lifted the mask to her head, pausing for a brief moment before sliding it on. "I'll see you inside."

Martin nodded. He would follow Ricki while his brother secured the female. Once Marvin was finished, he would follow. This gave them a better chance as well if something should go wrong. Then, there would be at least one of them that could come to the rescue.

* * *

A short time later, Ricki had slipped into the gathering of cloaked figures standing outside the magnificent entrance to the maze. She immediately recognized the image from the doors. It was only when the group parted that she saw Ristéard's proud features standing high above everyone.

Biting her lip, she clenched her fingers around the staff in her gloved hands. She wanted so badly to push through the group and go to his side. She needed to know if her parents were okay. She could see Sadao and Ajaska's heads once she focused. Surely her parents would be with them.

She forced herself to remember Martin's words to stay at the very end. It would allow him time to follow and her time to know what was going on. She took a purposeful step backwards when the procession began to move up the steps. Glancing over her shoulder, she could barely see the difference in the rocks behind her. It was only because she knew that Martin was there that she could pick out the slightly unusual shape. Turning back around, she slowly climbed the steps and disappeared into the dark entrance.

* * *

Ricki gripped the staff in her hands and tried to focus on her surroundings, but it was impossible. She had caught a glimpse of her mom and dad as they climbed the steps. It had broken her heart watching her dad carefully help her mom up the tall stairs. No one around them offered a hand, but at least they didn't try to hurt them either for taking longer to navigate the almost two foot high steps.

She had expected to be disoriented for a few minutes when she first entered the mountain, but the goggles she was wearing immediately adjusted to the dimmer interior. Making sure that she stayed to the back, she stared ahead trying to keep Ristéard in her view.

Crossing the narrow bridge, she felt a sense of déjà vu sweep through her. It was as if her dream was coming alive. She turned, looking back at the entrance. Her breath caught as she gazed back at the huge, narrow opening. Turning as if in slow motion, she swore she saw the ghostly figures from her dream moving around her.

"Emera...," Ricki whispered, staring at the large tapestry hanging from the wall.

She blinked several times as the sound of Ristéard's voice echoed in the chamber. Pushing forward through the crowd, she watched in horror as the woman struck him across the face. Fury burned through her, chilling her blood. Her fingers curled and she knew that the tips were glazed with ice on the inside of her gloves.

"How do you know of the sacred vault?" The woman asked harshly. "How did you discover this location?"

Reaching up, Ricki pulled the mask from her head as she stepped through the crowd.

"I told him," she replied in a soft, cool voice.

Chapter 21

Ristéard kept his arm wrapped firmly around Ricki's waist as he watched the mixture of men and women in the vast hall. He still couldn't believe that she, Martin and Marvin had followed them. His gaze swept to where the two Kor d'lurs stood against the wall near the entrance to the underground chamber. He would be having a word with them when this was over about not following his orders.

"Hey," Ricki murmured in his ear. "Quit glaring at them. They did the right thing."

Ristéard turned his head and brushed a hard kiss across her lips. "They disobeyed my instructions to get you to safety."

Ricki leaned her forehead against his and sighed. Yes, they had disobeyed his orders, but they had also made sure that she was safe. They didn't take any extreme risks and both of them had been there as back up for her.

"It worked out," she simply replied, turning her head back to the festivities going on around them. "This cavern was empty in my dream."

Ristéard heard the faint unease in her voice. Shifting even closer, he held her as they watched a group of young children retell the story of the First Empress of Elpidios. The graceful movement of their arms and the echo of their song rose and reverberated throughout the dining chamber.

* * *

Lyna, the Keeper to the Temple of the Empress of Elpidios, had been shocked when Ricki had ripped off the mask. Fear, anger, and disbelief crossed the other woman's face as she returned Ricki's icy gaze. When the woman raised the staff in her hand, Ricki had quickly yanked one of her gloves off. Her hand rose at the same time as the woman pointed the staff at her. Red met white as the charge from the Blood Stone was engulfed in ice.

With a flick of her hand, both the ice and the charge dissolved into a mist, raining brilliant red crystals down among those in the room. Lyna had slowly sunk to her knees, her eyes wide with disbelief and reverence, before she bowed her head.

He and the others had watched as if in slow motion as one after another sank to their knees until only he, Sadao, Ajaska and her parents were standing. Martin had slipped into the room and quickly cut through the bonds holding them. Ristéard had known immediately that the show had drained Ricki. He had pushed through the kneeling crowd and caught her as her knees started to give out.

"I thought I told you not to do that," he had muttered, holding her cradled against him. "I need water."

Lyna had glanced up at his demand. Rising, she nodded and motioned for him to follow her. Ristéard had ignored everyone else. His only concern was on Ricki who lay quietly in his arms.

* * *

He jerked back to the present when he felt her warm breath in his ear. "What are you thinking about?"

"I worry about you," he admitted. "When you do things like you did earlier, it takes a lot out of you."

He felt the sigh she released. "I reacted instinctively," she confessed, raising her hand to touch the bruise on his jaw. "I was furious with her for striking you."

His eyes darkened and he glanced back, relieved that the performance was finished. He wanted her. After today, when he thought he would never see her again, he realized that he wanted to grab every second for the rest of his life and hold her close.

Rising out of his seat, he pulled her with him. He nodded to Marvin and Martin to let them know to keep an eye on Walter and Nema who were clapping and chatting excitedly with the children from the performance. He just shot Ajaska an exasperated look when the Kassisan raised his eyebrows and laughed.

Turning, he gave Lyna a look that warned her not to stop him. "My Empress is tired and needs to rest," he said in a curt voice. "My men have set up our shelters in the outer chamber."

Lyna bowed her head in respect. "My people will guard the chamber," she promised. "Tomorrow, I will lead you to the entrance of the maze."

"Until the morning," Ristéard said, turning away.

Ricki glanced over at where her parents sat. "My parents…," she started to say.

Ristéard pulled her close to him. "They are fine," he whispered in her ear. "Marvin and Martin will make sure they are escorted safely back to the chamber."

Ricki frowned as she glanced around the large dining area. "Where's Sadao?" She asked. "I haven't seen him since right after dinner."

"He is probably scouting the area," he replied with a shrug. "The only one I am worried about right now is you."

Ricki glanced at him and he grinned. The rosy blush that spread across her cheeks showed that she finally understood what he meant. An answering smile curved her lips and she nodded, slipping her hand into his and squeezing it.

"I'm worried about you, too," she murmured.

Ristéard's eyes darkened until the silver in them looked like it had turned to liquid. The moment they turned into the long corridor leading to the upper main chamber, he pushed her up against the smooth wall. His hands wrapped around her wrists and he pulled them up over her head.

She opened for him, her lips meeting his in a heady kiss that stroked the fire burning inside him to a white-hot flame. For several long minutes, the kiss deepened as their tongues tangled and fought in a passionate dance. He released her hands and pressed his lips to the warm skin of her cheek before following the curve of her jaw to her ear. Their hands frantically ran over each other in an attempt to memorize the other.

"I love you, Ricki," he breathed against her skin. "I thought I would never see you again and for the first time in my life, true hopelessness threatened me in a way nothing else in my life has ever done. I have lived through a lot, but the idea of anything happening to you...."

His voice broke and he captured her lips again. He slid his hands up and tangling them in her hair. Her hands wrapped around his back, frantically searching for a way under his shirt to his skin.

With a muttered curse, he pulled back and swept her off her feet. Holding her close, he strode down the dim corridor to the chamber where Marvin and Martin had set up the shelters they had retrieved earlier. Crossing the room, he shrugged the cover over the doorway aside and stepped into it.

Carefully lowering Ricki to her feet, he grabbed the bottom of her shirt and pulled it up and over her head. His breath caught when he saw she was not wearing the cover over her breasts. Her nipples pebbled as he stared at them.

Her hair, which she had braided after bathing before dinner, hung down over her shoulder. He brushed it aside and cupped her breasts with his hands. Her loud gasp filled the tent when he captured one taut peak between his lips and sucked deeply on it.

He followed her down when her knees gave out and she sank down onto the soft bedding. His hands caged her beneath his body even as he continued his assault on her breasts. Her fingers worked frantically on the stays of his shirt, pulling each one free until it hung open.

A shudder ran through his body when her finger pinched his nipples. Releasing the rosy peak, he captured her lips again in a kiss that challenged her to meet his passion with her own. Their tongues fought, danced, and mated, in a ritual older than time.

Rising up away from her, he twisted and kicked off his boots and pants. She did the same, meeting him flesh on flesh as they both knelt on the bed. He groaned when she suddenly released her grip on his shoulders and lowered herself down until she was on her hands and knees. The position placed her even with his cock.

"Ricki," he groaned, threading his hands through her hair on each side. His fingers curled around the back of her head and he guided her forward. "That's it. Take me! Take all of me," he demanded in a guttural voice.

A choked cry escaped him when she did. He looked down and watched as she slowly slid his throbbing cock between her lips. This time there was no hesitation, no shyness. She took him like a woman that was starving. His breath hiccupped as he watched her take inch after delicious inch into her mouth.

He threw his head back when she began sucking on him. The feel of her hot, moist mouth wrapped tightly around him drove him crazy. A hoarse cry escaped him when she began sliding her mouth back and forth along his length.

Bending his head forward, he watched her suck on his cock. His balls drew tight and he tried everything he could to hold back his orgasm, but the erotic sight of his cock disappearing between her beautiful lips was too much. He called out a low warning, hoping she would stop. Instead, one delicate hand reached up and cupped his rock hard sack and she gently rolled it at the same time as she slid her mouth back around him.

He exploded down her throat. Instead of pulling back, she drank his hot seed while holding his heavy sack in her hand. One slender finger reached out and gently rubbed the smooth skin just below it. If he thought his orgasm had been incredible before, the unusual stimulation she added sent him into a new realm of ecstasy.

"Ricki!" He breathed out in a hoarse voice. "Oh, my Empress."

He was trembling by the time she leisurely released his cock. The last touch of her lips against the sensitive tip was so pleasurable, that it bordered on pain. His hands moved down to her shoulders, holding her so that she knew he wanted her to remain down on her hands and knees.

He ran his hands down along her back, before bringing them up under her to cup her breasts. Now it was his turn. He had not been lying to her when he said that Elpidios males were aggressive, or that they had a high sexual appetite. Tonight, Ricki had ignited both.

He pulled back just far enough to study the smooth lines of her back. Rising he released a low growl when she started to move. Her head lowered, but it was so that she could follow his movement more than out of submissiveness.

Her low cry of surprise echoed in the tent before she buried her face in the covers to smother it. A grunt of satisfaction escaped him as he pushed another finger into her slick vaginal channel. She had not been expecting him to press into her so aggressively to test her desire.

She was more than slick. Her own need dampened the silky curls between her legs until he could see it. Rubbing his fingers in it, he leaned over her, pressing his cock between her buttocks as he spread some of her slick juices over her nipples.

"Ristéard," she whispered hoarsely.

"Tell me you love me, Ricki," he demanded, pinching her nipples hard and holding them. "Tell me. When we get back to the palace, I am going to clamp your nipples."

She buried her face in the covers again when he released them. Blood pumped to the tips making them throb. Her body trembled when he leaned over her again. The feel of his cock, hard and ready again, pressing against her ass, made her both hot and nervous.

"I need you," she whispered brokenly. "I ache."

"There are things I want to do to you, Ricki," he whispered in her ear. "Things that will make you scream."

Ricki turned her head and looked at him. Her blue eyes had turned to the color of the mountain lakes, deep, and crystal clear. In them, he saw the curiosity.

"What kind of things?" She asked.

Ristéard smiled and stroked her pulsing clit with his fingers. Once they were slick with her juices, he slid them up along the line of her buttocks. Her eyes widened in shock when he pressed against the tight rosette of her ass.

"Wonderful things that will make you beg for more," he promised, straightening until he aligned his cock with her hot channel. "You will be mine in every way, my Empress. I will know every inch of your body."

* * *

Ricki smothered the groan in the covers again. His words drew a very vivid picture of what he planned to do to her. What she had not expected was that her lessons were to begin right then and there.

Ristéard's cock was fuller and thicker than she remembered as he pushed it into her. She breathed in deeply, holding back the urge to demand that he take her hard and fast. Her hips thrust backwards as he impaled her with his cock. It was as if he wanted her to feel every inch of it.

Her legs spread a little wider and she raised her ass in an innocent invitation. She had no idea that she was showing him that she was being submissive. All she knew was that she wanted more.

Her fingers curled in the covers when he began moving back and forth in a rhythm that made her want to scream. A shudder ran through her when he started to increase the speed, his hips striking with enough force that she could feel his cock touching her womb.

She could feel the pressure in her body building with each stroke. The hint he had given her earlier of what he wanted to do to her built in her mind until she thought she would die if he didn't show her what he meant. The thought of him possessing her in every way, sent her body spiraling out of control.

She felt his hands on her ass again, spreading the cheeks. Instinctively, she tightened the muscles. A surprised cry escaped her when she felt a stinging slap to her ass. She started to rise up, but stopped when she felt him rub the hot skin.

Pressing back against his hand, she moaned again when he pulled his cock almost all the way out. She rolled her hips, trying to tease him to push back into her. He did, but this time, he also pressed against the tight ring of her ass with his fingers. A low moan of pain escaped her when the pressure increased before his finger slid into her.

He continued the slow rocking of his hips even as he pressed a second finger into her ass. Only when she relaxed, did he begin to increase the speed of both his cock and his fingers. The double stimulation was too much for her over-sensitive nervous system.

A low, guttural cry escaped her as she shattered around him. Her body fisted and pulsed around his as she came hard. She could feel her vagina squeezing his cock, magnifying her pleasure. A moment later, his cry blended with hers as he exploded, pulsing his seed deep into her womb.

He waited until both of their bodies began to relax before he pulled his finger from her. Collapsing to the side, he wrapped himself around her back. His body, locked to hers, was still too hard to pull from her safely. He pressed a kiss to her shoulder as his cock continued to pulse.

"Ristéard," she whispered sleepily.

"Yes, my Empress," he responded, pressing another kiss to her shoulder. "What is it?"

"I love you," she said. "I… just wanted you to know that I love you."

Ristéard wrapped his arm tighter around her waist and pressed his hips upward. "I love you too, Ricki," he whispered. "I love you too, my unwilling Empress."

A smile curved his lips when she released a satisfied sigh. He could tell she had fallen into an exhausted sleep. It took several more minutes before he could safely pull from her body.

Once he did, he used the cleanser in his travel bag to clean them both. He knew she had slipped into a deep sleep when she didn't move as he cleaned her. Tomorrow, he thought. Tomorrow, we will hopefully find a way to save our world.

He knew that he still had a traitor to find, but he would deal with whoever it was once he returned. The Temple held enough of the Blood Stones to give them the time they needed to discover a way to fix their world. Hopefully, whatever was in the vault would help them permanently fix the problem.

Either way, on this world or on another, he and Ricki would have a life together. He wanted one without their children worrying if they would have a place to live. For he knew now, that wherever they lived, as long as Ricki was with him, he would have a home.

Chapter 22

Ricki glanced around her the next morning, taking in the beauty of the underground city. They had learned last night that Lyna and the others were direct descendants of the original workers who built the maze. They had split into two groups centuries ago, those that would eventually become part of Manderlin's people, and those that became the ghosts of the Eastern Mountains.

"A member of my family has been the Keeper since the first Empress left here," Lyna was explaining as she walked through the city. "It has been our responsibility to protect the maze and the vault until the Empress of Elpidios returned."

Ricki had discovered that almost sixty families lived in the underground city at any given time. She also learned that many of them left for a period of time when they came of age to mate with someone outside their clan to reduce the chance of inbreeding. The mates of those that left would either return to live their lives in the city, or they would return with their child. All that were originally not from this area were blindfolded so they would not know the location of the Temple.

"No one has located the Temple before you," Lyna admitted. "Part of the security of it comes from whatever is in the Vault. No equipment works here."

"That explains why all scans have come back negative," Sadao said with a nod. "Do you know what is in the vault?"

Lyna shook her head. "None knew, but the first Empress. She was the only one who ever entered the vault. It was said whatever was inside, only she could control."

"There are traps in the maze," Ricki murmured. "Do you know anything about them?"

Lyna stopped in surprise and nervously glanced at Ricki. She seemed to be debating whether she should tell them something. Ricki watched her face as a mix of emotions washed over it.

"I know there are traps," she reluctantly admitted. "When I was younger, two of my friends and I went down into the maze. We all knew that I would be the next Keeper to the Temple and I... Well, we discovered the truth behind the stories of the maze. On the first trap, one of my friends was wounded badly. If we had not been so close, she would have died," her voice faded as she looked around the families working together in the same marketplace. "I was young and foolish back then and learned a valuable lesson. Since then, guards have been placed in front of the entrance to prevent others, especially the children, from venturing into the labyrinth."

Nema stepped up and gripped Lyna's hand in compassion. "We were all that way once," Ricki's mom said in a soothing voice. "Walter is still that way, sometimes."

"You wish," Walter mumbled. "I wasn't the only one who was picking straw out of my ass."

"Dad!" Ricki gasped, staring at her father.

Nema grinned at everyone, even though her face had turned a nice rosy red. "Oh, yes, he was. I was always the smarter one. Straw is not soft," she retorted smugly.

Walter laughed and winked at Ajaska who was chuckling. "It was worth it. I had a rash on my ass for a week, but damn, it was good," he boasted.

"Oh my God," Ricki groaned, turning to Ristéard and leaning her forehead against his chest with a shake of her head. "Get me out of here. There are some things daughters should never know about, and their parent's sex life is one of them."

"Talking about sex life," Walter said bluntly. "What are your intentions with my daughter? Are you going to marry her?"

Ricki pulled back and glared at her father. "Okay, time to go," she snapped.

Ristéard pulled her back against him. Tilting her chin up, he stared down at her until she forgot everything, but him. A smile curved her lips when she saw the love in them.

"I love you, Ricki Bailey," Ristéard said, ignoring the others standing there. "I claim you as my Empress, before your father, mother, and witnesses. From this day forth, you will stand at my side as my partner. You are the Empress of Elpidios."

Ricki's lips parted and tears glistened in her eyes. While his words deeply moved her, it was the emotion behind them that captured her heart and soul. He was announcing to the world, to his people and hers, that she belonged to him. He was doing great until he tilted his head and looked at her with a scowl.

"Now is the time you accept me as your Emperor and admit my claim," he prompted.

Ricki shook her head and chuckled. "I accept you as my partner. I accept you as the Emperor of Elpidios," she retorted with amusement. "We'll talk more about the claiming part when we are alone."

"Oh, Ricki," Nema whispered, sniffing. "He sounds just like your dad did when he proposed to me."

Walter chuckled and wrapped his arm around his tiny wife. "I believe the words were 'I love you, damn it, we're getting married whether your dad approves or not'," he said with a grin.

Nema rolled her eyes up at Ricki and shook her head. "Daddy loved him," Nema admitted. "It wasn't as dramatic as he makes it sound."

Ajaska grinned down at Walter with a thoughtful look. "But it worked, yes?" He asked.

Walter looked up at Ajaska and nodded. "Of course it works. She's standing here, isn't she?" He retorted good-naturedly.

"Okay, I think it is time to get moving," Ricki interjected with a sigh. "Lyna, I'm guessing that the traps are real and to proceed with caution."

Lyna nodded, gazing at the unusual group. The Emperor of Elpidios, the mythical Empress returned, the Emperor's guard, a Kassisan, and four creatures unlike anything she had ever seen. As strange as it seemed, they had all been foretold in the prophecy handed down to her.

The Empress of Elpidios will return with an unusual army of her own. They will come from far away worlds and bring with them the skills needed to save Elpidios.

Lyna turned and guided them through the marketplace. On the other side, they continued down a series of passages and steps that led deeper under the mountain. At the end of a long passage, stood two guards.

She stopped just before she reached them. Turning to face the small group, she looked at them. Ricki knew immediately that Lyna would not go any farther with them. She saw the worried expression on the Keeper's face. Stepping forward, she held out her hands. Lyna hesitated for a moment before reverently placing her palms against Ricki's.

"Thank you," Ricki said quietly.

"May the first Empress guide you well," Lyna replied. Stepping back, she waved her hand at the two guards. They immediately stepped to the side. "The first trap is twenty paces inside. It is as far as I got. You must watch where you step. One of the stones on the floor is loose."

"What happens?" Ajaska asked.

"A spear of the Blood Stone is triggered," Lyna and Ricki said at the same time.

Lyna looked at Ricki, startled by her knowledge. "How…? Safe travels, my Empress," she said instead, stepping back out of the way.

Ricki put her hand out when Ristéard started to go through first. Shaking her head, she gazed into the dark recess of the stairs. Looking at him, she gave him a determined smile.

"I have to go first," she murmured. "I know what to do."

Ristéard's face tightened, as if he was about to argue with her, but instead, he reluctantly nodded in agreement. Ricki breathed a sigh of relief. She did know what to do, she hoped. The answers had been partially on the door and partially on the tapestry.

She couldn't help but admire the intelligence of the ancient people who built the maze. They gave the answers, but not all in one place. She had reviewed her notes earlier this morning while Ristéard was still asleep. If not for that, she might have missed the clues embedded in both.

Pulling her notebook out for future reference, she looked down at it. Penciled in neatly on the lines were each trap and how to bypass it. Biting her lip, she read the first one.

Count nineteen paces. Third stone to the left and fifth to the right trigger crystal spears. Follow steps on tapestry until step seven. Follow directions on door to trap two.

The tapestry had depicted the steps to missing the traps, while the door held the key to which direction to take in the maze. Drawing in a deep breath, she stepped forward into the darkness. Ristéard would follow her, then her parents, Ajaska, and Sadao. Marvin and Martin would take up the rear. She paused on the eighteenth step and studied the floor in front of her in the low, red glow cast by the crystals lining the walls.

"The entire mountain is made of Blood Stones," Sadao whispered in awe, running his hand along the smooth surface. "The mountain is the treasure."

"No," Ricki said, glancing at the symbols on the floor. "Whatever is in the vault is the treasure. The mountain is just part of it."

She started to take a step forward, but paused when she felt Ristéard's hand on her arm. She glanced over her shoulder at him and gave him a tentative smile. Laying her hand over his, she squeezed it in reassurance.

"Be careful," he ordered in a low, husky voice.

"I will. Everyone, make sure you follow in my footsteps exactly. If you don't… Well, if you don't, it isn't going to be good," she instructed, turning and following the steps she remembered from the tapestry.

* * *

Two tense hours later, they paused to rest. They had made it through four of the traps so far. She glanced at Sadao's pale face. Her heart melted at the pain in his eyes.

"I think you should return to the caverns above," she said quietly, watching as her mother fretted over both him and her father. "Marvin and Martin can return with you. Just remember to reverse the steps going back."

"I'll be alright," Sadao muttered, holding his arm.

Nema shook her head. "It's broken," she replied, looking back up at Ricki before turning her attention back to Sadao. "How many fingers am I holding up?"

Ricki rolled her eyes. "Mom, the stone hit his arm, not his head. I don't think he is in danger of a concussion."

"Nema is right," Ristéard said. "The brothers can return with you."

"No," Marvin and Martin both said at the same time. They had been silent throughout the journey until now. "Our place is with Ricki. She is the one we must protect."

"I will return with Sadao, Nema, and Walter," Ajaska interjected. "Marvin and Martin are right. You do not know what you will find in the vault. Their knowledge and abilities may come in handy."

Ristéard nodded. "Be careful," he responded.

"I'll give you my notes, in case you need them," Ricki said, tearing the page and handing it to Ajaska.

"What about you?" He asked when he saw that it contained the instructions for the next five traps. "You will need the others."

Ricki smiled and shook her head. "I always make duplicates and keep them in different places in case one gets damaged," she replied, pulling a separate, neatly folded piece of paper out of her shirt pocket. "It is the OCD in me."

"Ricki, I'm sorry, sweetheart," her father mumbled in a low voice.

Ricki knelt in front of her father and tenderly cupped his cheeks in her hands. Leaning forward, she brushed a kiss against one rough, whiskered side. She sat back and smiled at him.

"It isn't your fault," she whispered. "The steps were higher than we realized and the last one was slick from the water. I would have fallen too, if not for Ristéard balancing me."

It had been true. The fourth trap in the maze had been a difficult one to negotiate. Water ran down each side of the curving stairs making the steps slick. The key was not to touch the sides, a difficult task as it would have helped with keeping their balance.

What was not in the instructions was the stairs would be of varying heights, making it necessary to focus on each step. They were nearing the top when her father lost his balance. Ajaska had taken the position behind Nema in case she needed assistance, while Sadao had stepped behind her dad.

Her dad's hand had brushed the wall as he started to fall. Sadao had grabbed her dad, but the movement had also put him in harm's way. A thick slab of crystal shot out, striking him in his right arm as he pushed her dad upward.

The blow had hit him just right, breaking his forearm. He would have fallen if not for Martin grabbing him. Martin had helped Sadao the rest of the way up the narrow staircase.

Ricki saw her dad glance at her mom's pale face. The journey was becoming more difficult the farther they traveled, and the traps more elaborate. Her mom's petite height and the physical demands were taking a toll on her. She dropped her hands and picked his up, squeezing them in encouragement.

"Think of mom," she murmured. "Think of what it would do to her if something happened to you. Then, think of what it would do to you if something should happen to her."

Her dad's face reflected his resignation. "Just remember what it would do to both of us if something should happen to you, Ricki," he added gruffly. "You'll always be our little girl."

"I know, dad," Ricki replied. "I'll have Ristéard, Marvin, and Martin with me. Go with Ajaska and Sadao. I need to know that you will be safe."

Walter nodded. "If I start to fall on the way down, just get the hell out of the way," he said, walking by Ajaska and Sadao to Nema. "I'll meet you at the bottom."

Ajaska chuckled, but his eyes remained serious as he turned to Ricki and Ristéard. "I'll make sure they get back safely," he promised.

Ricki watched as her parents, Ajaska, and a very pale Sadao walked slowly back the way they came. Drawing in a deep breath, she turned when they disappeared down the watery steps. She nodded to Ristéard to let him know that she would be alright. They had six more sections of the maze to negotiate.

Six more traps to make it through before they reached the vault. There would be no stopping until they did.

Chapter 23

Ristéard held Ricki's shaking body. A low curse escaped him as he gently helped her to sit down on the uneven floor. He turned and murmured for Martin to get him some water and an energy bar.

"You are doing it again," he complained teasingly.

Ricki laid her head back against the uneven walls. Here the walls were left in their natural state. Ricki suspected the reason was due to fewer workers being allowed in the sections closer to the vault.

She tiredly looked around the huge chamber. They had just made it through the ninth trap. A shudder ran through her as she thought of it. Rock climbing had never, ever appealed to her. While she was fine going up, it was the coming back down part that paralyzed her.

She blinked when she felt Ristéard warm hand brushing the loose strands of her hair back from her cheek. He held up the flask of water to her lips, holding it for her. Only when she pulled back did he lower it.

"Have I told you how proud I am of you?" He murmured tenderly. "You've tackled these task with the same determination as you did when you climbed that tree to get away from me."

A dry laugh escaped Ricki as she remembered that night not so long ago. So much had changed, she thought wearily. Gone was her neat, orderly little world. Thinking back on it, her entire life had been turned upside down from the moment they left Earth.

"If you were to ask me a year ago if I thought I would end up living on another planet, I would have laughed at you," she said with a weak smile. "If you were to ask me if I thought I would end up being mistaken as a prophesized Empress saving a dying world and traversing through a maze filled with deadly traps, I would have pointed you to the nearest mental hospital."

"And if you were to tell me that I would fall in love with a beautiful alien who takes my breath away with her beauty and courage, I would never have believed it either," Ristéard said, caressing her flushed cheek with the back of his hand. "It just goes to prove you never know what will happen in the future."

"Unless you are an fortune-telling Empress from another world," Ricki chuckled. She looked over where Marvin and Martin were quietly talking. "Where do they come from?"

Ristéard glanced at the brothers and shrugged. "I don't know," he admitted. "I don't think anyone does. The only thing known about the Kor d'lurs are their natural curiosity about the worlds around them. They are a highly advanced species is all I can tell you."

Ricki shook her head and took a bite of the power bar. "If the people of Earth knew that there were really aliens out in the star systems, they would probably freak out," she observed. "Especially if they found out that they had actually visited Earth and that there were still some there."

"Yes, from what I've heard, they did not handle it very well," he agreed.

Ricki slowly turned her head and looked at him with a shrewd, assessing stare. Leaning forward, she touched his arm. A dark frown creased her brow when he tried to avoid her eyes.

"What are you not telling me?" She demanded.

Ristéard shifted uncomfortably before he released a sigh. "You know that Elpidios has recently joined the Alliance council, correct?" He asked.

"I think I've heard that mentioned a few times. Ajaska is part of the Alliance Council as well, isn't he?" She asked.

"Yes," he replied. "I have only had a few reports, many of them weeks or months old. My priority has been trying to find a solution to the problems on my world, not others. The only reason I joined with the Alliance was in the hopes that additional help and resources could be provided to find a solution to the radiation destroying Elpidios, and for potential places for my people to relocate."

"Okay, I understand your reasoning to join the Alliance, but what does that have to do with Earth?" Ricki asked in exasperation.

Ristéard looked at Ricki. "Your world has been sending out signals for close to a century. It was decided by the Alliance that they had reached a level of advancement to be contacted," he said slowly.

Ricki was silent for several long minutes as she thought of what he was telling her. She knew about all the satellites and probes that had been sent out. Still, she honestly didn't think that anyone really expected an answer. Her troubled eyes rose to his and she saw the truth in them.

"First contact," she whispered. "How… How did the people of Earth take it?"

Ristéard released a long breath and sighed. "About as well as you would imagine. The Alliance sends in an advance group of warriors known as the Trivators. They will soon have the Earth back under control. They are there to establish calm, but I must admit that I do not envy them their task."

Ricki nodded, stunned to think of what the Earth must look like now. Something told her that she and the other members of the circus were much better off than if they had been back home. She slowly finished the power bar, even though she was no longer hungry.

* * *

It took another hour to finally get to the last section before the vault. She wiped a dirty hand across her cheek. The path had been littered with large sections of fallen crystal. Sadao had been right, the entire mountain was made from the Blood Stones. It seemed the deeper they traveled into the mountain, the denser and brighter the crystal grew.

"I need to rest for a minute," she admitted, sinking wearily down on a large section of the crystal.

Ristéard handed her the flask of water that he had replenished at an underground stream they had crossed shortly after they started on this last leg of their journey. Sitting down next to her, he nodded to Marvin and Martin when they announced they would like to analyze a section of the crystal that looked slightly different than the rest.

"What is the next trap?" Ristéard asked, taking the flask from her outstretched hand and drinking deeply from it. "It is the last one, correct?"

Ricki knew he wasn't going to like what she had to say which is why she avoided mentioning it. She nervously tucked a strand of her hair behind her ear. Across a thin bridge of crystal was the huge doors leading to the vault. Her eyes roamed over it, taking in each minute detail.

She opened her mouth to respond when she heard a noise behind her. Turning, she rose in surprise. Her hand instinctively moved to Ristéard in warning.

"What is the next trap?" A familiar voice asked with a crooked grin. "You didn't write down how to get past it."

Ristéard turned slowly, his face stiffening and his gaze cooling. He ignored the pain of betrayal as he stared back at the figure standing behind them. His eyes flickered to where Marvin and Martin lay unconscious on the floor of the large chamber. Long darts containing what he suspected was a powerful sedative protruded from their necks.

"Why?" He demanded, looking back at the man he considered his brother. "Why, Andras? Why would you betray me? Why would you betray your world?"

* * *

Andras looked coldly back at Ristéard. The why was easy to answer. He wanted enough wealth to leave this miserable, dying world. His family had made a fortune from the Blood Stones before he was born. The problem came from his uncle. Alcolsis had been jealous of the wealth his grandfather and father had amassed over the decades. A falling out between his grandfather and Alcolsis had made him an outcast. Andras hadn't minded. Even as a boy, he recognized the difference between the way his family lived and that of the others in his village.

What his father hadn't realized was that Alcolsis would build an even greater wealth, by gathering followers who listened to his lies. His uncle had risen quickly, quietly killing those who resisted him, while building a steady following of those who believed in his empty promises.

Andras had been ten when Alcolsis had returned to the village of his birth. He had gleefully killed his grandfather and cast Andras' family into the underground city with the others that resisted him. It had taken years for Andras to understand why his uncle just didn't kill them. Alcolsis knew that breaking the will of the resistance lay in breaking the men, women, and children. You could not do that in death. Death made them a martyr.

"I've hated this world my entire life," Andras said, pointing the weapon in his hand at Ristéard. "It was dying, so why should I care one way or the other how fast?"

Ristéard started to step in front of Ricki, but stopped when Andras shook his head. His eyes flickered to Marvin and Martin, hoping that the Kor d'lurs bodies wouldn't be affected by whatever drug had been used.

"Do you really expect to get away with this?" Ristéard demanded in a low voice. "Others will know what you have done. I know what you have done. For that alone, I will kill you."

Andras laughed and shook his head. "I did a little research before I came down here," he explained. "Those two are practically impossible to kill, but they can be drugged as long as you take them by surprise. By the time they wake, the four of you will be trapped inside this chamber, buried just like the treasure hidden in the vault. The treasure that will be my ticket off this world."

"Lyna and the others will stop you," Ricki said angrily.

Andras shook his head again. "I'm afraid that my followers have imprisoned them, along with your parents in the city above. I must remember to thank the Kassian Ambassador for giving me the key to getting to you. Of course, it helped when I threatened to kill your parents."

"You bastard," Ricki snarled, trying to break free when Ristéard grabbed her as she stepped forward. "You are a horrible, horrible excuse for a man."

Andras amused laughter echoed in the large chamber. "I believe I've heard you say the same about Ristéard," he chuckled before growing serious. "I don't have time for your temper tantrums, Empress. What is the key to getting pass the tenth trap and opening the vault?"

Andras watched as Ricki's face twisted into a mask of rage. He had been expecting this type of resistance from her, which is why he hadn't knocked Ristéard out. He figured he would need to use his former 'friend' to encourage the human female to do what he wanted her to do.

"Go to hell," Ricki hissed, clenching her fists at her side.

Andras watched warily as ice coated her fingertips. "I wouldn't," he warned, not pausing as he fired a shot into Ristéard's leg.

Ricki cried out when she felt Ristéard stumbled backwards from the force of the blast. She twisted and caught him as he started to fall. Pain glittered in his eyes and in the tightness of his jaw, but he didn't make a sound as she helped him to the ground. Blood was pooling at an alarming rate under his upper thigh. A dark, scorched area peeled the cloth of his trousers back.

"Ristéard," Ricki whispered, frantically trying to stem the blood flow. Tears of frustration blinded her when she realized that she wasn't strong enough to tear the material of her shirt. "I need to stop the blood."

"Don't," he whispered, closing his eyes. "You have to escape."

"I'm not leaving you," she whispered, closing her eyes and placing her hand over the wound.

A pulse of ice shot from her palm into the wound. The ice hardened, freezing the blood. She opened her eyes when she felt Ristéard's hand wrap around her wrist to stop her.

"Don't," he ordered, realizing he was already too late when she swayed. "You haven't drunk enough water."

"I'm okay," she insisted, reaching up to brush her fingers against his cheek. She froze when she felt Andras behind her. "Don't!" She warned, swiveling to look up at him.

"The next shot will be to his stomach," Andras informed her coldly. "It can take hours to die from such a wound without medical help."

Ricki rose to her feet, ignoring her trembling limbs. Her fists clenched again. She was too drained to form any ice. Her body was dehydrated from their journey and her lack of appetite. The little water she had drunk wasn't enough to replenish her.

"Please," she begged, glancing back at where Ristéard lay with his eyes closed. "He needs medical attention."

Andras laughed harshly. "As you can see, that isn't available. It won't matter anyway," he said. "Now, the tenth trap. How do we get past it and open the vault?"

Ricki drew in a deep breath. Her eyes flickered to the narrow, crystal bridge in front of the massive doors to the vault. Drawing in a deep breath, she knew she would have to go along with Andras until she could find a way to stop him.

"The bridge is part of it," she whispered. There is a line down the center. You have to stay on it."

Andras nodded, staring at her. "Then, I suggest you lead the way," he said. "I'll follow. And, Ricki…" He paused, waiting to make sure she understood exactly what he was about to say. "I learned from Ristéard the best way to take my time killing someone. Once I'm done with him, I'll start on you."

He watched as her throat worked up and down. The small nod of acknowledgement was the only other response she gave him. Turning on her heel, she walked toward the bridge.

* * *

A lone figure stood in the shadows watching as almost two dozen men held those in the center room locked down. He had followed the group, picking up on the transmission between them. His eyes searched the area for two specific men. A frown creased his brow when he didn't see them. Instead, he focused on the two small figures that had been brought to the front.

His lips tightened when he saw one of the mercenaries raise a weapon and point it at the tiny woman's head. His fingers curled in an effort to keep from reacting too soon. He couldn't help them, if he was captured as well. He had traveled a long way to find what he was looking for and wasn't about to risk losing it.

He recognized the tall Kassisan standing off to the side. He had minor interactions with him from time to time over the past year. The huge male shrugged off the hands restraining him and held up a piece of paper. Whatever was on it, it appeared to satisfy the mercenary because after he looked at it, the male turned on his heel and walked away.

A menacing smile curved Rime's face. Slipping into the shadows he worked his way through the empty carts littering the main marketplace. He needed to speak with the Kassisan.

* * *

"You shouldn't have given him the paper," Nema fretted, winding her hands together. "What if he hurts Ricki? Oh, Walter, what if he hurts our baby girl?"

Walter pulled his trembling wife into his arms and held her tightly against his body. He cursed the fact that she would be able to feel him shaking as well. When Andras had threatened to kill Nema, it had scared the life out of him.

"They are way ahead of him," Walter said soothingly. "Plus, she has Marvin and Martin. There is no way anyone can hurt those two."

"Nema, why don't you sit and rest," Ajaska suggested. "Walter, is right. Ricki has the two Kor d'lurs. They are very protective of her."

"So am I," a voice behind them stated coldly. "Who is he and why is he after my daughter?"

Ajaska shifted to the side. He had caught a glimpse of the Glacian as he slipped into the lower chamber. He recognized Rime's huge shape almost immediately.

"Your... Your... Who in the hell are you? And who is your daughter?" Walter stuttered, glaring suspiciously at the tall man with the eerily familiar blue eyes.

"Ambassador Rime, from the Glacian star system," Rime replied. "Ricki is my daughter. I have been looking for her ever since the Coalition agreed with the Alliance about contacting Earth. I tried to get there before the Trivators arrived, but I didn't make it. By the time I arrived, Earth had turned into a war zone."

"What the hell are you talking about?" Walter asked, glaring back and forth between Ajaska and Rime. "Why are you saying Earth is a war zone?"

Ajaska grimaced and cast an apologetic glance at Walter and Nema. "I meant to tell you about that," he said with a sigh. "But, now is not the time." He turned to Rime. "Can you get some of those weapons that Lyna and the others use?"

"Of course," Rime replied, starting to turn. He paused when Nema stepped forward and touched his arm.

"Is it true?" She asked quietly, searching his cold, hard face. "Are you Ricki's biological father?"

Rime's gaze focused on the soft brown eyes staring up at him. He had made the right decision twenty-four years ago to leave Ricki with the two tiny humans. His throat tightened when he thought of the danger she was in. If he wasn't careful, he might never get to meet her.

"Yes," he replied in a curt voice. "I'll return shortly. Do you know where the bastard was going?"

A cold, hard look came into Ajaska's eyes and he nodded. "I'll come with you," he said. "You'll need my help to get through the traps set up. We'll need to get to him before he reached the fifth one, I haven't been through it or the others." He turned and looked down at Sadao's pale face. Andras had struck the man in his broken arm when he tried to protect Walter and Nema. "Watch over them," he ordered.

"Always," Sadao replied, struggling to stand up. "Ajaska…"

Ajaska paused in the shadows of a large cart. "Yes?"

"If Ristéard doesn't kill Andras, make sure you do," Sadao said in a cold voice. "What he has done deserves no less."

Ajaska stood still for a fraction of a second longer before he nodded. Turning, he followed Rime. The former Star Ranger moved in the shadows as if he was one of them. Ajaska decided it might not hurt to do a little more research on the Glacians. They were a very talented bunch to have on his side.

Chapter 24

Ajaska nodded to Lyna. He and Rime had worked their way around until they found where two of Andras' men were holding the Keeper and her guards. Rime's silent elimination of the men reaffirmed his conclusion that he needed to have a serious talk with the Glacian.

"How do you do that?" He asked under his breath. "The ice thing."

Rime's lips curved up at the corner. "It's genetic," he replied.

"Well, damn," Ajaska muttered in disappointment, using one of the new words he had learned from his human friends. Turning, he looked at Lyna. "Can you and your guards take care of the others?"

Lyna twirled the staff in her hands. Her chin lifted as she glared back at him. From the cold smile on her face, it didn't look like she would have any trouble.

"The male, Andras, claimed to be friends of the Empress," Lyna replied stiffly. "I will not believe so easily next time."

"Let's go," Rime growled. "The longer we take, the farther ahead Andras will be."

Ajaska nodded. The two of them slipped through the narrow area, once again using the structures scattered about as cover. The few men that Andras had brought were not covering the lower areas. It was obvious that Andras considered the men expendable.

What concerned him was that the male must have another exit plan.

"The only exit plan he'll have is being dead if I have my way," Rime replied in a tight voice to Ajaska's softly spoken thought.

"So, how is it you have a half human daughter?" Ajaska asked, glancing over his shoulder. "I thought it was forbidden for any member of the Coalition to be on a primitive planet."

Rime glared at the back of Ajaska's head. "It's a long story," he snapped. "And a personal one."

Ajaska shrugged as they stopped just before the first trap. "When this is over, I'll buy you a drink and you can tell me it," he offered. "Make sure you do exactly as I do or I'll be having that drink by myself."

Rime grimaced as he watched Ajaska navigate the stones. "Just keep in mind who just saved your ass," he said, following. "Oh, and I might warn you I have very expensive tastes."

Ajaska broke into a steady jog, now familiar with their path. "Why does that not surprise me?" He muttered, slowing as they approached the next trap.

* * *

Ristéard focused on the sound of Ricki's footsteps. He knew what Andras was capable of, after all, they had trained together since they were ten. What he had not expected was his former friend's deviousness. Now, small things that had happened over the years began to make sense.

Andras family had been quiet, withdrawn, during their years in captivity, yet Andras had sought him

out. There had been two occasions when he had been
with Andras when he had almost died. Both times,
Andras had been with him, before disappearing. The
first time had been when a narrow footbridge made
from wood and rope had snapped as he was going
across. Andras had been in the lead, but had stopped.
He had told Ristéard to go ahead, that he would catch
up.

The bridge had snapped when Ristéard was half
way across it. He had managed to grab hold of one of
the wooden planks that made up the bridge. He had
eventually pulled himself up. The next day, he had
returned to look at the bridge, but Andras' father had
already replaced it.

He stumbled upon the remains of the rope from
the bridge several months later. It was obvious one
side had been partially cut through. Andras' father
had said that he used part of the rope elsewhere
which is why it was cut, but Ristéard knew the man
was lying.

The next time was when they were climbing up
one of the rock faces to a higher level. Andras had
been ahead of him and went over the ledge before he
made it to the top. A large boulder at the top came
loose and crashed to the floor of the cavern they were
in. If he had not noticed an easier way up the side and
shifted his direction, he would have been in line with
the boulder and killed. Andras had peered over the
side shortly afterwards and joked that he had missed
Ristéard by just a few inches.

Other times washed through him. The issues with the shields the most recent. Andras had been hinting that perhaps Emyr or Harald were to blame. He was the one who suggested that they be reassigned to deal with the unrest in the former councilmen's zones.

Andras had also wanted to go with them on this journey, but Ristéard thought he would be better suited finding the traitor who was sabotaging the shields. No wonder Jarmen was having issues finding the problem. Andras could stay one step ahead, by making the issues look random and fixing the issue before Jarmen arrived.

Touching his leg, Ristéard grimaced at the pain. Ricki had slowed the bleeding, but it would need to be stopped. Sliding the small laser knife out of the sheath at his waist, he pressed the button on the handle to extend the heated blade.

Looking down, he raised his head just high enough to be able to see the wound. He moved the blade over the area and pressed it against the torn flesh of his thigh. His head fell back against the hard crystal floor as the sickening scent of burning flesh reached him. He stared up at the ceiling, his jaw hurting from the force of keeping any sound from escaping him.

It took several minutes for the pain to dim to a dull, steady throb instead of the shooting agony it had been. He retracted the blade, keeping it in his hand as he rolled onto his stomach. From his position, he could see Ricki as she carefully walked across the long narrow bridge. Andras followed her, he was mindful to stay back several feet.

"What now?" Andras' voice echoed in the chamber.

Ricki had her back to him. She was gazing up at the massive doors. After several long seconds, she turned to look at Andras.

"I'm not strong enough to open the doors," she admitted. "The first Empress must have been pure Glacian. She used ice to expand the locks. It has to be done correctly for the locks to disengage."

Ristéard's jerked when Andras struck Ricki across the face. The blow knocked her back against the doors. Her body slowly slid down them when her knees gave out under her.

"Wrong answer," Andras snapped. "I've seen what you can do."

Ristéard was about to rise when he saw Ricki struggling back to her feet. His hands pressed against the floor to push him up when he felt a presence behind him. Rolling, he stared into a set of familiar blue eyes set in a very unfamiliar face. His eyes flickered to the man kneeling next to the stranger.

Ajaska's silver eyes stared back at him with cold determination. The long darts that had been embedded in Marvin and Martin's necks were clenched in his fist. Ristéard glanced back at where Ricki stood. Her hands were pressed against the door.

He knew that she would try to open the doors. He worried about what it would do to her. Just the small bursts of ice that she had done had drained her. He feared something of this magnitude would kill her.

"Ricki," he whispered in a husky voice. "If she tries to open the doors, it might kill her."

"What is she trying to do?" Rime asked.

"I'm not sure, but I think it has something to do with ice," Ristéard said hoarsely. "We have to stop Andras."

"Is there another trap?" Ajaska asked, quietly.

Ristéard nodded. "Yes," he replied, bowing his head. "There is a line in the center. We have to stay on it. The bridge will collapse otherwise."

Ajaska nodded. "Rime and I will go," he said, starting to rise.

Ristéard shook his head. "No," he said in determination. "I will go. See if you two can wake Marvin and Martin. Don't let Andras know you are here."

Rime looked around. A grim smile curved his lips. He didn't need to use the crystal bridge, he could make his own with ice.

"You distract him," Rime instructed. "I'll make my own bridge and get across. Ajaska, you try to wake up the Kor d'lurs. I haven't come this far to lose her now."

"Lose her… Who are you?" Ristéard demanded, glaring at the male who was ordering him around.

Rime turned to look at Ristéard. "My name is Rime. Ricki is my daughter," he said quietly.

* * *

Ricki glared at Andras. Her right hand was pressed against her heated cheek. It pulsed from where he had struck her.

"I'm telling you, I can't do it," she said, using the door to help pull her to her feet. "I can make a small amount of ice, but nothing like what it would take to move the locks in the door."

Fear flashed through her when he pointed the weapon in his hand at her head. Ricki stared back at him, waiting. They both turned when they heard Ristéard's harsh voice call out.

"Andras, don't," Ristéard said. "Let her go. She is telling you the truth."

Ricki tried to jerk away as Andras shifted. A low cry escaped her when he reached out and pulled her in front of him before he turned to face Ristéard. She bit back another pain filled cry when his fingers tightened on her arm in warning.

"That's far enough," Andras warned. "You are just as resilient as ever, I see."

Ristéard's face froze into a calm mask. "None of your assassins could kill me, what makes you think you can?"

Andras lifted the weapon in his hand and pressed it against Ricki's temple. Ricki trembled as she looked back at Ristéard. Her fingers clenched and she could feel the familiar tingle on the tips of them.

Her eyes narrowed and she glanced down, before raising her eyes to his again. She saw understanding dawn in his eyes before they shifted back to Andras.

Her breath caught when she saw him grimace as he stepped off the bridge.

"I'll kill her," Andras bit out in a cold voice. "You know I will."

"If you do, then you'll never get the locks undone," Ristéard pointed out, knowing he was right.

Andras took a step back toward the door. "You're right," he said, pulling the weapon away from her temple to wave it at Ristéard. "Move…"

Ricki reacted the second the weapon moved away from her head. Her hand flew up, her palm directed over her shoulder and at Andras face. His loud curse echoed in the chambers as a burst of ice flew into his eyes.

Ricki darted forward into Ristéard's arms. The flash of the hot blade leaving Ristéard's hand flew by her. She turned in time to see it embed in Andras chest at the same time as he fell forward. Her eyes widened at the long shafts of ice protruding from his back.

Turning dazed eyes to the man walking up from behind Andras, she gazed into eyes the same color as hers. She trembled and backed up as he came closer. Her fingers instinctively searched for Ristéard's when he wrapped his arm around her waist.

"Who… Who… are you?" She whispered, staring at the man.

Rime paused several feet from where Andras' body lay. Ice still coated his fists. Raising them, she watched as the ice dissolved into a mist. Her head turned and she watched as Ajaska, Marvin, and Martin slowly crossed the bridge.

"My parents?" She asked, staring at Ajaska.

"They are fine," Ajaska assured her.

The man standing in front of her glanced over at Martin and Marvin. He knew they didn't realize that he had seen them all those years ago. They were the ones he had originally been hired to bring in. It had taken some serious hunting to find the real criminals behind the slayings on the Service Port. Only when he had proof the two Kor d'lurs were not responsible had the bounty on their heads been revoked.

"Thank you," Rime said, nodding his head.

Martin gave him a reluctant smile. "It is we who should thank you. The least we could do was watch over your daughter," he replied.

"The bounty?" Marvin asked.

"Revoked almost fifteen years ago," Rime responded.

Ricki glanced back and forth, frowning. "Wait a minute," she whispered. "Daughter? Whose daughter?"

Ristéard's grip on her tightened when the stranger took a step closer to her. Ricki was thankful for his support even as she worried about his leg. The trembling that had started earlier from the rock climbing blossomed into full blown shakes as shock began to set in.

"My daughter," Rime replied in a solemn voice. "You are my daughter, Ricki. Your mother was a human woman I met. She was killed shortly after you were born by some radical humans who suspected I was not from your world. I wasn't able to save her, but I did find you. I stole you away from them. I wanted to take you with me, but I knew where I was going it would be too dangerous for a baby. I had a lot of enemies at the time that would do anything they could, to get to you. I also had to take into consideration the Coalition, which rules my world. Earth was considered a primitive planet and was considered off-limits, even if I was on assignment. I would have been instructed to eliminate any Earthlings I came into contact with since we did not have the technology at the time to erase the memories of those we came across like we do now." He paused for a moment, drawing in a deep breath as he stared down at her. "I knew you would be different. I needed a place where you would be accepted for who you were," he explained quietly.

"What... What is your name?" She asked hesitantly.

Rime stepped forward, unable to resist touching the daughter he thought he would never see again. His fingers skimmed her soft cheek. She looked very much like the woman he had fallen in love with when he was a young Star Ranger.

"My name is Rime. I'm Glacian," he said. "You look just like your mother did when she was your age."

Ricki's eyes filled with tears. She swallowed over the lump in her throat as she stared at the man, the alien, who claimed to be her father. Gripping

Ristéard's hand tightly in hers, she pushed past her grief that her biological mother was dead and she would never know who she was.

"What was her name? What was my mother's name?" Ricki asked in a voice thick with emotion.

Rime smiled down at her. "Ricki," he told her with a sad smile. "Ricki Strickland. She was from Bentonville, Arkansas."

Ricki gave Rime a watery smile. Now she knew who she was. She was Ricki Rose Strickland-Bailey and she was half human and half alien. Turning in Ristéard's arms, she wound her arms around his neck and buried her face in his chest and cried.

Chapter 25

"Are you sure this will work? Ricki asked, looking up at the massive doors. "The prophecy says a woman with blood of ice."

"Well, we can always put a wig on him?" Marvin suggested.

Rime glared at the Kor d'lur who grinned back at him. Ricki just rolled her eyes, thankful that the two brothers had removed Andras' body from in front of the doors. Of course, the fact that they threw it over the edge of the crevice had been a rather tense moment.

She grinned at Martin as he ran an imaginary zipper across his lips when Rime turned his intense stare on the other brother. They had been picking on the Glacian for the past hour while they waited for her to finish crying and get herself back under control.

They had also bandaged Ristéard's leg while he whispered to her. She smiled up at him when he pressed a kiss to the top of her head. She had wanted him to rest, but he insisted on seeing what was in the vault.

"I am the Emperor of Elpidios," he reminded her gruffly. "This is what my family and countless others have spent centuries searching to find the answer to."

"The answer was under your nose all this time," Ricki reminded him.

Ristéard released a heavy sigh and nodded. "True, but the key to understand it was not."

"Neither was the skill necessary to open the doors," Ajaska pointed out. "Rime, are you ready?"

"Yes," Rime replied, glancing up at the massive doors. "Ricki, explain to me what I need to do again."

"Place your hands on the imprint," she said. "Then, slowly release the ice. It will flow through the narrow tubes that make up the locking system. As it expands, it will release the locks."

Rime nodded, glancing up. "Sounds simple enough," he said quietly.

Ricki watched as her biological father concentrated. Ice formed, flowing from the tips of his fingers and spreading up the long tubes. As it reached the first set of connected circles it wound around them. The moment it touched the second set, the first set opened. Ricki, Ristéard, Ajaska, Martin, and Marvin all took several steps back to watch the impressive display.

"It's a star chart," Ricki murmured. "Look, see the star systems? And, those look like constellations."

Ajaska and Ristéard both released a low curse, while Martin and Marvin stared up at the image with concern. Ricki glanced at the brothers, noting their serious expressions. Her eyes opened wide when the last lock disengaged and the doors began to slowly open. Rime pulled his hands away and stood in front of the doors as they opened inward.

Ricki gripped Ristéard's hand tightly in hers as she stepped forward to stand next to him. Her loud gasp echoed through the chamber as the brilliant light of red poured through the doors and surrounded them. She started when she felt Ristéard's hand pull her forward with him as he started to walk through the doors.

"What is it?" He breathed, staring at the huge red form that looked suspiciously like a spaceship.

Martin and Marvin followed behind them. Their eyes glued to the large Crystal Ship. They had seen only one other during their travels. The ship was used to travel through space… and time. Not many existed outside of the realm they had briefly visited.

"It is a living ship," Martin answered quietly. "It must have been trapped here all this time. The crystals growing and reproducing until it sealed itself in the mountain."

"A living ship?" Ristéard asked, walking around the structure. "What… Where did it come from?"

"My world," Rime replied in a quiet voice. "Or I should say the world where my people came from originally. It is said my people traveled in such ships, moving through different dimensions. We encountered an unknown species that followed one of the ships back to our galaxy. The species…. There was a great battle and our world was destroyed and with it the crystals that you call Blood Stones. A few scatterings of survivors spread out around the star systems in an effort to escape them. Only Officers of the Star Realm were given a Living Ship to pilot. The First Empress must have been part of the SR. She escaped and hid on Elpidios, but then some of the creatures must have tracked her down. She knew she had to prevent them from obtaining the ship, so she hid it inside the mountain."

"How long will it continue to produce crystals?" Ricki asked, walking up to the ship and touching it.

Rime looked at the ship, then at the crystals forming the walls. It would spread out continuously. He wouldn't be surprised if the crystals weren't already forming under the surface of all the mountains in the region.

"Forever," Rime replied. "Your technology won't pick up the crystal if it is covered this deep. You would need someone who could connect with it to get it out of here. The Officers of the Star Realm could physically link with the crystal ships. Each officer was embedded with a Nano-computer in their brain according to the history I've read. This technology was abandoned when the last Living Ship was lost. You would need someone capable of doing that to move the ship out of here. Once it is outside and no longer confined, the crystals will reproduce even faster," Rime replied.

Ristéard scowled as he looked at the ship. "Are there any officers like that left?" He asked, staring up at the pulsing ship.

"No," Rime said, shaking his head. "At least, none that we know of."

"I know someone who could tap into it," Ajaska replied with a smile.

"Who?" Ricki asked, turning to look at Ajaska with a frown.

"Jarmen," he replied. "He would be able to control it."

"We can help him," Marvin and Martin said at the same time.

Ristéard looked at the ship. "Now that we know where the crystals are from, we can use it to heal my world," he said as a large smile curved his lips. He turned to Ricki and pulled her against him, ignoring the pain in his leg as he held her close. "You did it, my Empress! You have saved Elpidios."

Ricki's laughter was cut short as he captured her lips with his. Winding her arms around his neck, she returned his kiss. She might have started out as his unwilling Empress, but she was definitely ready and willing now.

"Does this mean we get to go back to the palace now?" She whispered when he slowly broke the kiss.

Ristéard's eyebrow rose at her question. It was only when he saw the dark desire burning in her gaze that he remembered their last conversation about when they got back. His own eyes darkened to molten silver and he felt his body harden.

"Soon, my Empress, soon," he promised.

* * *

Ristéard distractedly nodded his head at Jarmen's technical explanation. Martin and Marvin had spent the last two days dismantling the traps leading down to the vault. Jarmen had joined them early this morning. He had been fascinated by the Living Ship, running his hands over it with an almost reverence.

"I believe I am ready to connect to it," Jarmen said. "I will return with it to the location set up just outside of the city. The Rues will be leading the research. I believe they will be of sufficient help in understanding the history of the crystals. From what I have learned, the ship absorbs the radiation and converts it to food. The by-product are more crystals. The Rues have theorized that the ship was absorbing the radiation and continued to do so, but when it became completely trapped inside the mountain, it could no longer receive the needed food to reproduce at the levels it had before. Deposits of the crystals from the vault alone are enough to stabilize your planet for the next five millenniums if the crystals remain on your world."

"Make sure that it is secure," Ristéard ordered. "I do not want anyone taking it."

"That is highly unlikely," Jarmen replied. "I am the only one who has the capability of connecting with it."

"How long before we know for sure that this will save my world?" Ristéard asked, gazing back at the glittering ship.

"A noticeable reduction should be detected within days, normal levels within a month with the amount of the deposits available," Jarmen replied, his eyes glowing as red as the ship as he processed the information. "Less than a year for all environmental resources to stabilize and return to normal."

"Thank you for the information, Jarmen," Ristéard answered, his voice fading as Ricki stepped across the bridge with her parents and Rime. "Make sure that you share it with the other scientists."

Jarmen's eyes returned to normal. For a moment, he studied Ristéard's face before turning to look at Ricki's glowing one. A look of puzzlement crossed his face as he tried to process the emotions they were feeling.

"What is it that you feel for Ricki?" Jarmen asked suddenly.

Ristéard glanced at the unusual man and smiled. "Love," he said simply. "I feel love when I look at her."

Ricki looked up and smiled. Her eyes softening as she returned Ristéard's steady gaze. He started toward her when Jarmen's calmly murmured words hit him. Stumbling to a stop, he turned and stared at the man in disbelief.

"What did you say?" He asked hoarsely.

Jarmen frowned and gazed back at Ristéard wondering if he had said something inappropriate. "I said she is reproducing. Is that not the appropriate term for a woman who is carrying a child?"

Ristéard ignored Jarmen's question. His eyes glittering fiercely with pride and possessiveness. He had his home back and now he had his family. His Empress had saved more than Elpidios, she had saved him.

Opening his arms, he buried his face into her neck as he wound his arms protectively around her. A shudder escaped him as he drew in deep calming breaths.

"Are you okay?" Ricki whispered in concern, running her fingers through his thick hair. "Ristéard, are you alright?"

Ristéard pulled back and gazed down into Ricki's worried eyes. A smile curved his lips and he brushed a kiss against her lips. Losing himself in her brilliant blue eyes, he saw something he hadn't seen before, he saw a future.

"I'm thinking about kidnapping you," he whispered.

To be continued…. **Jarmen's Jane Doe**

If you loved this story by me (S.E. Smith) please leave a review. You can also take a look at additional books and sign up for my newsletter at http://sesmithfl.com to hear about my latest releases or keep in touch using the following links:

Website: http://sesmithfl.com
Newsletter: http://sesmithfl.com/?s=newsletter
Facebook: https://www.facebook.com/se.smith.5
Twitter: https://twitter.com/sesmithfl
Pinterest: http://www.pinterest.com/sesmithfl/
Blog: http://sesmithfl.com/blog/
Forum: http://www.sesmithromance.com/forum/

Excerpts of S.E. Smith Books

If you would like to read more S.E. Smith stories, she recommends Hunter's Claim, the first in her Alliance series. Or if you prefer a Paranormal or Western with a twist, you can check out Lily's Cowboys or Indiana Wild…

Additional Books by S.E. Smith

Short Stories and Novellas
For the Love of Tia
(Dragon Lords of Valdier Book 4.1)
A Dragonling's Easter
(Dragonlings of Valdier Book 1.1)
A Dragonling's Haunted Halloween
(Dragonlings of Valdier Book 1.2)

A Dragonling's Magical Christmas
 (Dragonlings of Valdier Book 1.3)
A Warrior's Heart
 (Marastin Dow Warriors Book 1.1)
Rescuing Mattie
 (Lords of Kassis: Book 3.1)

Science Fiction/Paranormal Novels

Cosmos' Gateway Series
Tink's Neverland (Cosmos' Gateway: Book 1)
Hannah's Warrior (Cosmos' Gateway: Book 2)
Tansy's Titan (Cosmos' Gateway: Book 3)
Cosmos' Promise (Cosmos' Gateway: Book 4)
Merrick's Maiden (Cosmos' Gateway Book 5)
Curizan Warrior
Ha'ven's Song (Curizan Warrior: Book 1)
Dragon Lords of Valdier
Abducting Abby (Dragon Lords of Valdier: Book 1)
Capturing Cara (Dragon Lords of Valdier: Book 2)
Tracking Trisha (Dragon Lords of Valdier: Book 3)
Ambushing Ariel (Dragon Lords of Valdier: Book 4)
Cornering Carmen (Dragon Lords of Valdier: Book 5)
Paul's Pursuit (Dragon Lords of Valdier: Book 6)
Twin Dragons (Dragon Lords of Valdier: Book 7)
Lords of Kassis Series
River's Run (Lords of Kassis: Book 1)
Star's Storm (Lords of Kassis: Book 2)
Jo's Journey (Lords of Kassis: Book 3)
Ristéard's Unwilling Empress (Lords of Kassis: Book 4)
Magic, New Mexico Series
Touch of Frost (Magic, New Mexico Book 1)
Taking on Tory (Magic, New Mexico Book 2)
Sarafin Warriors
Choosing Riley (Sarafin Warriors: Book 1)

Viper's Defiant Mate (Sarafin Warriors Book 2)

The Alliance Series

Hunter's Claim (The Alliance: Book 1)

Razor's Traitorous Heart (The Alliance: Book 2)

Dagger's Hope (The Alliance: Book 3)

Zion Warriors Series

Gracie's Touch (Zion Warriors: Book 1)

Krac's Firebrand (Zion Warriors: Book 2)

Paranormal and Time Travel Novels

Spirit Pass Series

Indiana Wild (Spirit Pass: Book 1)

Spirit Warrior (Spirit Pass Book 2)

Second Chance Series

Lily's Cowboys (Second Chance: Book 1)

Touching Rune (Second Chance: Book 2)

Young Adult Novels

Breaking Free Series

Voyage of the Defiance (Breaking Free: Book 1)

Recommended Reading Order Lists:

http://sesmithfl.com/reading-list-by-events/

http://sesmithfl.com/reading-list-by-series/

About S.E. Smith

S.E. Smith is a *New York Times, USA TODAY, International, and Award-Winning* Bestselling author of science fiction, fantasy, paranormal, and contemporary works for adults, young adults, and children. She enjoys writing a wide variety of genres that pull her readers into worlds that take them away.

CPSIA information can be obtained
at www.ICGtesting.com
Printed in the USA
BVHW041447100119
537521BV00015B/247/P